SONS OF ATLAS

Daniel J. Nesher

Seacross Publishing

ISBN Ebook: 9781737046899
ISBN Paperback: 9788987203613
ISBN Hardback: 9798987203620

Cover Design by: Daniel J. Nesher

Seacross Publishing
Https://www.seacrosspublishing.com
seacrosspublishing@gmail.com

Printed in the United States of America

My writings are dedicated to my wife who has loved me unconditionally through the years. And to my one and only son. They are my heart, my life, and my best friends.

"You're as rich as your imagination and faith make you."

CONTENTS

CHAPTER 1: AT HOME AT SEA

A thunderous clap and then a deep hard thud hit the ship. A young boy of thirteen bolted straight up in his bed. He was in a small bunk bed in a very small room deep below decks. When he sat up he smacked his head on the wood of the upper bunk.

"Ouch!" he exclaimed loudly.

But the ship was fully engaged in some sort of battle and the noise outside was way too loud for anyone to have heard him. This time he sat up much slower and as he lowered his feet to the floor he was startled by the water that now filled his room up to his knees. He stood in shock. The water was cold and pierced his legs like shards of glass.

Boom, crack, crunch.

The ship rocked and lunged and he lost his balance. The water moved too so much so, his bedroom door burst open and also off the seams. A larger rush of water forced its way in. Now he was thrown off his feet. He sort of swam but also was pulled by the next surge of water but this time out of his room and out into the cargo bay. The bay was dark and full of violence. The beasts in cages cried out in fear. Men were everywhere preparing for battle. They were moving in hast to the armory and then up the large circular stairs to the upper deck. One large man with a long mustache that arched around his face and down to his chin had a long strange rifle in one hand as he approached the boy.

He kneeled and with fear in his eyes called out, "Hanno, you have to get to the balsas!" And with that, the man grabbed Hanno and started pulling him through the cargo bay. Now out in the open, Hanno was orienting himself. The water was up to the large man's thighs and when he pulled the boy by his shirt, Hanno was partly floating as he was pulled. He was on his back floating and he could see holes in the upper deck letting in pieces of the violence from above. It was dark with bursts of light everywhere. It could have easily been a horrible storm but then he remembered the men with weapons and knew it was an attack. When they got to the stairs, the man stood him upright and placed Hanno's hands on the rails. The man locked eyes with the boy.

"Hanno for the love of your father and all that is in heaven, save yourself." And then he exploded upward clearing a path. The spiral staircase appeared to be made of some sort of metal and also fine wood. It was wide enough for two to walk side by side. But the large man and Hanno were the last to come up. Water poured forth from above. Splashing and hitting both of them. At one point a rather large flow even knocked the man off his feet. Hanno caught him and they both continued upward. Hanno looked down and saw the water was not only coming down from the opening above but also up from below so that now the whole of the cargo bay was full of water. He looked for a moment on the creatures with sadness but was jerked by the man upward.

Out on the upper deck it was like coming out of a foxhole. There was lightening, smoke and dark storm clouds above. And explosions of light and fire all around them. Suddenly a large dark faced man with an even darker cloak all around his head and body seized him. He was grabbed by arms all about him, but his face was completely dark. It wasn't really even a face so much as it was a dark deep nothingness. A black hole within the hood of the cloak that looked more like red smoke mixed with a dark red light. And in the center of the darkness were deep red eyes. The black cloaked man drug Hanno away. Then the large man and ten of his companions came to Hanno's aid. There was explosions of fire and light. There was slashing of blades and blood. And suddenly he was free. Hanno ran to the edge of the great ship. He looked out over the edge and could not understand what he was seeing. The sea and sky were mixed and there was no telling which way was up and which way was down. But with another huge explosion behind him, he was blown from the upper deck and thrown far.

Beep….Beep…beep…beep…

Up close an electronic screen was blinking through a blue green mesh of material. It was flashing an alarm showing the time 5:45 a.m. The area of the alarm was coming from what looked like a cocoon hanging from the underside of a house. The house was up on stilts creating a space under the house. The cocoon unraveled and now could be seen as some sort of hanging hammock. Out from the meshed hammock the boy from the ship emerged. He was slightly older. The alarm, a holographic display, was coming from an electronic device under his skin attached to his wrist.

When he stood he was much taller than he was in the dream. He had that awkward look a teenager has when they grow up too fast. His hair was shaggy but also curly long and black. The kind that sticks up as much as it makes his whole head look like a hair helmet. His skin was brown and rugged. Most of his body and looks resemble Polynesian or Caribbean. He was unique and very few looked like him. He is so lean and tall combined with the shape of his huge hair head, he almost looks alien like. He tapped his wrist then tapped his right ear.

"Play Heathens."

Then we hear with him Twenty One Pilots

Heathens song play. Hanno was wearing nothing but a pair of surfing shorts. He threw on a beach day button down shirt that looked like it had seen better days. He unhooked the hammock and folded it up. From a nook at the edge of the lower side of the house, he pulled out a backpack. He shoved the hammock into a pocket and slung the pack on his back. Then leaning up against the stilt that was surrounded by a small batch of shrubs he pulled out an antique cruiser bicycle. As Hanno road out from the under the house he road along a trail that went along the inner coastal inlet. There was a whole row of houses on stilts. Some clearly that had been flooded recently. Out of the neighborhood he found himself up on a small road that led to the highway. As he rounded the corner at the last house he stopped for traffic. Then he looked up. Up in the sky was the great city of New Atlanta. A floating city that span along the East coast from the old city of Atlanta all the way up to what used to be Raleigh North Carolina. The center of the great city was somewhere near the North and South Carolina border. Hanno couldn't remember all of the history but from school he had learned that after the war to end all wars, the world had to be rebuilt. The emergence of new technology combined with changes in social and political structure, led to the development of five floating city states throughout the world, three in the Americas. He lived in the shadow of New Atlanta.

On the ground was where the working class and the poor lived. Titles and wealth may have changed hands, but the age-old separation of the ruling class and the working class held firm. He rode along an old highway next to the inlet. Above, the city was hanging like a man made paradise, shiny and clean. Down below the "grounders" lived and worked. Some were allowed in the city by day but only if they had a work visa. Most of the workers had to leave by nightfall. The city did not push up to the coast but was set back. After all even though the wealthy may not visit the ground often, they still want a day at the beach.

The sun was rising over the Atlantic. Hanno rode his bike past the grounders mart and then turned east and up over the bridge that led to Surf City. The bridge rose up high over the inlet. Even at this early hour, there was still lots of working class folk on their way to work. The grounders were not allowed to live at the beach either. But like in the city above, they would have to commute over the bridge to their jobs as waitresses, housekeepers, and cooks. The road was full of makeshift vehicles; renewed older models held together by new tech. There was a black SUV with some sort of future looking large steam boiler built into the roof. It had pipes, tubes, and wires going in all directions. It most was running on recycled garbage. The steam that came out was clear and clean. Then there were the packs of three wheeled motor bikes with mounted solar converters. They worked great out here on the edge of the great city. But anywhere under the city you had to run on gas, battery, or steam.

Right then a huge 28 passenger shuttle bus cut right suddenly. Hanno almost had to ditch his bike and jump off the bridge but was able to stop in time. The bus was open to the sky from half way up. There were all sorts of working grounders riding to work visible in the bus. The hood over the engine was missing too. And the engine had pipes, wires, and sparks of energy throughout. The roof was replaced with a thin new metal that was taken from the floating cities scrapes. The makeshift roof was enough to keep out the sun but not enough to keep out the rain.

At the bottom of the bridge was a security checkpoint just above the roundabout. Here all grounders had to show their work visas before they were allowed on the island. Hanno stopped in a line of pedestrians and bicyclers but still had to be checked through. As he waited in line he looked out and back at the floating city. Up and to the south of the ground bridge was a sky bridge that came down from the city. It was clean and made of the same new metal that was scrapped on the shuttle. The metal was strong but also transparent. The sky bridge at one end connected to the city and floated along with the city. But as it neared the ground huge piles and piers reached from the sky to the ground. These too were made of the new metal. Although transparent the massive size still made them completely fill the surrounding view. One went right down into the former town of Wilmington. And the other into the inner coastal water alongside the ground bridge. The sky bridge wrapped slowly and elegantly around to another arrival point to the island farther south. There were no check point's there, only electronic sensors and an invisible shield that prevented grounders from going up it. There were no lines and no backed up traffic. But synchronized driverless vehicles that moved along the beautiful road. As one would arrive at the beach the shield would quickly and automatically turn off as the vehicle cleared and then back on again. Then the occupants would disembark and the vehicle would disappear into the ground for storage.

Hanno cleared the check point and made his way south to the pier. As he rode, there was a clear division of those who came from the sky and those who worked for them, their clothing, their manner, and their separation as they walked. The sky bridge ramp was closer to the pier where all the beach shops and restaurants were. Hanno passed a group of sky teenagers. They had on the latest new clothes and styles. They were clean. Their hairstyles were curled, cut and unique. Hanno noticed a beautiful strawberry blond girl. She was about his age. She was uniquely cute but a little skinny. She smiled with a deeply shy manner about her when she locked eyes with Hanno. She was with the group but sort of behind the group, like maybe she was someone's younger sister. When the others of the group looked at Hanno, they were clearly laughing and one even took a picture with their wrist device. He didn't really notice until he saw the change in the girl's face when she realized he was not one of them.

Hanno stopped at the entrance of the pier store. The store hadn't changed its appearance in a thousand years. Oh of course it had new wood and new utilities. But the look was a real draw of the tourists for the nostalgia.

Atop the store a sign read, "Salty Tallywhacker."

Hanno walked his bike along the wooden deck outside the store. There was a large glass window along that side. He looked at his reflection, at his long hair and long slim body. His arms went below his waist and his long legs grew out of his surfer shorts. He thought who would ever find him attractive. But then the smell of the sea caught his nose. He pushed the bike around back and placed it in a storage shed. He dropped his shirt and grabbed his boogie board and was off to the ocean.

He almost ran right up into the waves and then launched onto the board. The only place he felt at home was in the ocean. Here his long arms and legs made his paddling smooth and fast. One wave after another he rode. His joy was full upon his face. As his board and body were one with the waves. Then the movement in the ocean froze in time. In slow motion as Hanno flew on a wave, he was using his long feet and legs to guide him turning with the wave's energy. For a moment portions of his legs and feet that were in the water, changed. The color of his skin slightly changed to a bluish grey and just for a moment it looked like something came out of his legs that were helping him move. But then the crash of the wave made it impossible to see exactly what was happening.

Soon others were arriving at the beach for the day. Hanno returned his board, put his shirt back on and then put on an apron. It read, "Salty Tallywhacker" across the front.

A large bald man with a white goatee beard was working with customers at the front counter. Hanno went right to work stocking shelfs in the store.

"Hanno make sure to hang more t-shirts and Hawaiian shirts at the front."

Hanno's hair had dried way too fast for how he had just left the water. He finished his shelf and then brought a box to the front. Seth Vandergriff had gotten the pier store from his father. It was a family business going back before the war. And he had looked the part. Somewhere between a fisherman and a pirate. He wore a beach shirt with no sleeves. It had blue and white flowers all over it. He was in his sixties. He had an eagle tattoo on one shoulder and a sea turtle on the other. He would often tell Hanno.

"The eagle was to remember his buddies

who died in the war. And the sea turtle was to remind him of his father and the sea."

"I can only work till 3:00 today."

Hanno was hanging a bunch of t-shirts.

"How was the surf this morning?"

Hanno's eyes lit up, "The waves weren't super strong but they had some curls forming." Hanno stepped over toward the counter and they both were looking outside.

Then they both said, "Any day in the sea is a good day for me."

CHAPTER 2: A GIRL NAMED MOON

Midway School was named for the second Midway battle of the thirtieth Century. It was also designed to be midway between the sky and the ground. It allowed for grounders to receive a good education without any lowering of community safety. Of course the politicians meant for Sky people safety. There were six such schools that surrounded the massive city state. One on the West, two to the North, two to the south, and Midway which was toward the East Coast somewhere over what was formerly known as the piedmont of North Carolina. There were a number of sky bridges from New Atlanta to the ground. Hanno waited at a train stop near the one on his side. The train stop landed right at the Cape Fear River. What was once known as Wilmington had now been turned into a huge port for those from New Atlanta going to the beach. The trains were also made of translucent metals which allowed for a very pleasant view of the river, the ocean and the whole east coast as you traveled back and forth. There were all sorts of nice shops and restaurants at the port too. Hanno had to ride five miles to a ground train that then took him to the port. Hundreds of grounder children waited with him for the train. Some of them he knew but many he did not. The ride was truly a treat. Up, up, up they all went. Past the clouds and up to the school. The train instead of running on automated roads hung from a translucent track like an advance roller coaster might. With the track and the train all being translucent it really did make you fill like you were flying. It was a cruel thing for the grounder children to taste a part of sky that they would never be allowed to partake in, not fully.

Arriving at the school was nothing new to the children. The school was so large it better resembled a large university. On one end, the grounders arrived and made their way to class. On the other side of the school was the sky bridges that brought the children from New Atlanta. These children were from many races, backgrounds, and ethnicities, but all had one thing in common, wealth and position. The leaders did not believe in private schools for the need to indoctrinate all children in the ways of the Bliss. BLISS stood for Belief and Life in Science Scale. Originally a thought experiment started in the twentieth century from an obscure Psychology Department in Manchester, United Kingdom. But after the war adopted and ratified as the law and religion of the sky cities.

Since they were above the clouds all of the court yards, halls, and classrooms had retractable roofs. Open most of the year but closed in the winter. Hanno had changed into his school uniform but still had on his beach shirt over top. Although the uniforms were the same, the difference in quality and cleanliness was still visible. The group he had seen the day before was walking across the court yard from him. Again the same girl saw him and sent him a friendly smile. This time he scowled at her, having believed she was "in" on the joke the others had made about him. Her sadness with the rebuff was visible to all. A tall pretty girl saw it.

"Moon wants to smooch the grounder."

Another jumped in, "Might catch the Eagan's disease if she doesn't watch out."
Eagan's disease was a plague that hit the survivors of the war. It was proven to have come from a fungal pathogen that lived in the soil. But in fact many of the past bacterial and fungal pathogens such as tetanus, botulism and anthrax all came from the soil. But to those that rarely touched the ground, it was forgotten. It became another point to reinforce their condescension. Moon just followed the girls from her neighborhood. But she watched Hanno as he walked alone towards the hall.

Day after day their world this routine

repeated itself. Sky children coming from their protected world above. And grounder children being lifted up from their world below. Hanno and Moon walked from their separated trains along their separate paths to school. Then one day on the first day of a new semester the pattern changed. As Hanno unloaded his bike from the Train he saw her again. She was sitting at the end of a bench that looked out over the sea. As he waited for class to begin he watched her. She was reading something. A closer view revealed that she was reading an old copy of a small New Testament bible. She was concealing it with her school books. She was also being very guarded constantly looking back at the security cameras at the school.

Hanno approached her, "Whatcha you reading?"

She quickly closed and hid the bible in her schoolbook, "Oceanography." She lied.

"Oh yeah I'm in Oceanography too."

"I've got to go."

She got up and headed to class. He slowly followed her wondering why she was so paranoid. Maybe that's just how she was.

Hanno walked into the large lecture room. It held easily two hundred kids. The children were assigned seats and were marked as attended when their wrist device synced with their seat. Hanno touched his wrist device and his seat was highlighted for his eyes only. School was one of the last truly segregated spaces. It was rare for a grounder to mix with sky children socially outside of school. From time to time you would hear about a family who fell from grace due to some violation of the Bliss or some failure at finance. They would have to move to the ground. But never, and I mean never, would a grounder ascend to the heights of the city above.

Hanno took his seat. He tapped his wrist again and up in front of him was a holographic screen visible only to him. The professor was a kind attractive woman in her thirties. She stood at a stage preparing the lecture. She had on an English looking pants suit with a red vest. Although there was assigned seats, there was always hacks. One of the blond males that had made fun of Hanno sat two seats over from him. Two cocky loud boys who were with him quickly swiped at their seats below, but then moved up next to him.

One of them just said to Hanno, "Move over dude." Very rudely.

Hanno moved one seat over. At the top of Hanno's screen read the title of the class, *Oceans, tides, and everything in the sea.* He had really been looking forward to this elective. Last year's course on physics was taught by Professor Shendo and he really liked that. Now she was teaching this course on his favorite topic. Shendo put up on all of their screens but also on her overhead screen the currents of the world's oceans.

"Seventy one percent of the earth's surface is covered with water. And an estimated ninety seven percent of all the water on the earth, comes from the ocean. Do you know how many oceans there are?"

The blond haired boy tapped his wrist and a light lit up over his head.

He answered, "There are four, the Pacific, the Atlantic, the Indian, and the Arctic oceans."

Both Moon and Hanno clicked their wrist at the same time.

Shendo saw it, "Oh do we have more? Did he miss any?"

Moon answered, "Well actually the Ocean is one global ocean that stretches and connects throughout the globe. The divisions mentioned by Brody were labels early oceanographers used to distinguish regions."

Shendo looked to Hanno, "Anything to add?"

He just shook his head, "I was going to say the same thing."

This time Moon and Hanno shared a genuinely kind look. Then she quickly turned her head back toward the professor.

Shendo continued, "The world of the ocean is vast and unique. It has mountains and trenches bigger and deeper than anything we know about on land. If you put Mount Everest in the Pacific's Mariana Trench, the mountain wouldn't even break the surface."

All of the students were taking notes and coping

articles as the professor taught. Brody and his brood were talking nonstop. When the students tapped their wrist it connected them with the class audio system for a moment so the class could hear their questions and answers. But without that, up this high in the class, the professor could not hear them.

Brody turning to the others, "Swim team try outs start today at 4:00. I'm a shoe in for the 200 meters butterfly."

Then his friend added, "Sure you'll get first seat in the 100, 200, and any other you try out for. I'm just hoping to make the team."

Brody then said, "Last year we took the city championship. And this year I plan on leading the team to another first place trophy."
The boys were getting louder and more excited. Hanno was having trouble hearing the teacher. The professor had just asked a question about sea creatures.

Hanna hadn't even noticed when Moon was answering, "Of course Sharks, Dolphins, and sea turtles are everyone's favorite, but I find the Cephalopod's the most fascinating."

"Why's that?" asked Shendo.

"It's their ability to camouflage using chromophore cells. Each cell contains multiple types of pigments allowing them to…"
Right then Hanno pretended to stretch and accidentally on purpose bumped one of the boy's wrists connecting them to the class mic.

Brody can be heard to say, "I'd love to see Ms. Shendo try out for the swim team. I bet she has a nice a..."
The whole class laughed out loud. The boy cleared his mic and all of them looked hard at Hanno.

He just looked at them and said, "Maybe I'll try out for the team. I'm a pretty good swimmer."
Shendo looked at her screen then hit a code. Brody's wrist lit up with a red color. He knew what it meant. Trip to the Headmasters office. He stood and gathered his things.

Then to Hanno he said, "The day you make the team is the day I die."
Then he left. Normally Hanno didn't mind the bullying and treatment by the sky kids. But today it hurt on two levels. One, the look Moon gave him when he interrupted her answer. And two the thought that he wasn't welcome on the team. But he always had been alone and he wasn't going to let a little bullying stop his efforts.

The Olympic size pool was really amazing. It was indoors but open to the sky. It had bleachers made of the same translucent metals. And the pool was also made with this material so it looked like you were swimming in the sky. Students and coaches started entering the pool area. Some parents and students showed up and sat in the bleachers to watch the tryouts. Midway's swim team was celebrated as champions for the whole eastern region of the city. Brody was one of the first to arrive. He had a very muscular and long body. Clearly a long linage of swimmers in his family. When Brody and the other kids came out of the locker room they all looked like swimmers. They had on new suits and new swim hats. When Hanno came out of the locker room, he looked so skinny and long. He had on his surfer shorts and a long sleeve surf shirt. He had no swim hat and his hair stuck out and up in all directions. As the swimmers lined up on their lanes. His hair stuck up above all of the uniform white hats that covered the other boy's heads. He was the only grounder trying out.

One of the boys made fun of his hair saying, "Damn son that mop on your head is going to drag too much water. You need a cut bad."
He ignored him even though Brody and several others got a kick out of the comment. He saw Moon in the stands and decided he would get the courage to try again and say hi. He wrapped a towel around his neck hoping to hide his shallow small chest. Moon hadn't recognized him but when she saw him she lit up. He sat down on the row below her. Even though from a distance she looked nerdy and skinny. Up close she was well proportionate and very attractive. Especially to Hanno.

He said, "Hey Moon."
She shyly responded, "Hey."
Even though it was super easy to stalk someone you liked on-line, she was a lady and didn't let it on that she had tried to find out everything she

could about him too. But it wasn't uncommon for grounders to have very little on-line.

"I'm Hanno, I'm in your Science class."

"Oh yeah I recognized you. What a great class right."

He smiled, "Yeah totally I love Ms. Shendo."

"Hanno that is such a unique name. Where's it from?"

"I don't really know but I like to imagine I was named after Hanno the Navigator a 5th century explorer."

She flipped up a screen from her wrist and looked up the reference. Then downloaded a link about the explorer. He looked onto her screen and leaned in with his face close to hers.

Then pointed and said, "See he mapped much of the coast of Africa thousands of years before the coast was sunk after the earthquake of 3105."

She looked at him so close and her cheeks turned brighter than her hair. Then the moment was interrupted by Brody throwing his backpack down at her feet and his towel right at their faces.

"Hey scrub watch my stuff."

Then to Hanno, "I thought you wouldn't have the rocks to show up and try out."

He left as quickly as he came.

Moon apologetically just said, "My older brother."

Hanno shook his head, "You're kidding me. That sucks for you."

He made her laugh.

"Why are you named Moon?"

She answered, "I'm named after one of my ancestors. She was a hippie in the State of California when it was the land of Movie stars."

"That is so cool. I can't believe they used to make all the movies there. How did they shoot them in the desert?"

She just said, "I don't know I think they used lots of digital affects."

"Hey maybe we should connect in case I have a question on homework?"

It was an obvious move but a welcomed one.

"Yeah sure."

She lifted her wrist toward him as a women might have done thousands of years ago to receive a kiss on the hand. And he took her hand and lifted it as if that's exactly what he was going to do. But then held it and turned his other wrist upside down and over hers. The devices synced and small screen icons of their faces switched between the devices showing the connection.

"Third call for the 200 meter Butterfly!" The speaker blurted out.

"I've got to go. See you later?"

"Good get them."

She meant to say, 'Good luck, go get them." But it came out all wrong. She was embarrassed but also taken by her new friend. The swim team coach was at the starting line. There were several administrators and other instructors helping as well. Coach Pricket was walking the line with a digital clipboard.   He was an older coach and possibly semi-retired but helping the head coach with the tryouts. As he approached each swimmer he would call out their name. It would lock their identity from the school roster. He would then log them into the lane they were standing on. Brody was next to Hanno at lane 5.

"Name?"

"Brody Cadel."

When the device heard his name it found him and a small icon showed up. Coach Pricket then moved him to lane 5. Brody then stepped up on the starting block. He touched something below his ear and a small semi-visible shield formed as ear plugs and clear electronic eye goggles. He readied himself. Then the Coach approached Hanno. He looked him up and down with curiosity and slight disgust.

"Name?"

"Hanno Wilson."

The coach logged him into lane 6 but before locking it in, looked at him. Hanno stepped up on the starting block.

"Are you going to swim with your shirt on?" Hanno just nodded hopping no one would mind. Coach Pricket looked back at the Head Coach who was watching the whole event. Coach Dean approached.   His stomping footsteps could be heard all the way down the line.   All of the swimmers stood up and everyone in the stands were watching now too.

Coach Dean looked at Hanno, "Son your gunna have to take off your shirt."

Hanno gave in and slowly took off his shirt. His long lean upper torso and long arms looked bizarre. Brody and several other boys laughed.

Coach gave them a look and yelled, "Everyone on the line!"

But it never surprises me when the eyes of love can be blind to their object of affection. And Moon was enamored with Hanno. From her view there was something beautiful about him. When others saw skinny long lines. She saw smooth beautiful skin. When they saw big floppy hair. She saw clean, curly and gorgeous. As she looked at him stretching and preparing she noticed a circular tattoo on his upper left chest. No maybe it was a birth mark. But it was too well designed and detailed to be naturally formed.

But then when the Coach yelled out, "On your mark."

He bent at the waist and she could no longer see it.

"Get set."

Boom.

The sound of the electronic gunshot rang out and the boys launched off the starting blocks. All of the boys were swimming underwater before coming up on their first stroke. They all dove in with their hands and arms in front of them. But Hanno had his hands and arms down along his side. His hair seemed to almost form to the back of his head and streamline with the water. He was moving like a dolphin, flipping and kicking in rhythm. Although all of the boys launched out farther than him he quickly passed them. When Body came up for his first stroke, Hanno was seen underwater moving so fast he was half the pools length in front of him. Brody was too busy now stroking but everyone in the stands could see it. Hanno didn't even come up for a stroke or for air on the first length of the pool. When he reached the wall instead of the swimmers flip he just sort of instantly changed directions barely touching the wall. It didn't even look like he turned as much as his whole body changed directions. Then he was back swimming under water. This time about half way back he was passing the whole line of boys going the other direction. He came up for an awkward head to the side breathe and then back under water. His arms stayed to his side the whole way. Everyone in the stands noticed how fast he was going but they were joking and making fun of his swimming style. Moon watched closer. In the semi-visible translucent pool sides she could see from her position at the lower benches something. It looked like his legs and arms changed color and also shape. There was also a jet of water coming out the back of his legs. It reminded her of something. Then he was at the wall again and instantly changed directions heading back. He went so fast that he had passed the other boys coming of the wall finishing their first lap when he was heading to the finish. The coach saw his time and both Coach Dean and Pricket looked at the digital time with their mouths open. Hanno touched the finish and then stood in the pool with a huge smile and caught eyes with Moon. She was smiling too but also looking again at the circular markings on his chest. He noticed and got out of the pool and put his swim shirt on. The other boys came in and Brody had a record breaking time but all of that was forgotten knowing that Hanno had beat him. The stands had emptied out and all of the parents and students were arguing and yelling.

Over the mass noise were statements of, "He cheated!"

"He didn't do it right!"

"He didn't even Butterfly it's the 200 meters Butterfly!"

Hanno sunk beneath the moans and shouts of criticism. It was too much. His head dropped and from Moon's view all she could see was his curly hair from behind as he sulked away amidst the protests. Her compassion for him was full on her face. She stood to see over all those that were yelling and arguing. As he left back into the locker room the coach was assuring everyone that Hanno's time did not count. But all of that noise disappeared as Moon watched him. The Olympic size pool was contained in an arena that was lower than Midway High school. But because of its design the whole pool and arena hung magically over the ocean. Over Moon's shoulder in the narrow access stairs that led back up to the school, stood a mysterious man. He too was watching Hanno. He was dressed in an all black suit. The suit was an older looking one with bow tie, black and white checkered vest and long black outer coat with tails. He had a hat that was similar to a fedora but sharper. That type of hat was custom of the time for New Atlanta. And under the hat he wore a thin head covering that covered the sides of his face and the back of his neck. His dress would have been recognized as possibly a high level official, a powerful executive, or a priest in the Bliss. The nobles of the time would often dress in honor of the Bliss in a similar manner. He pulled from his inner pocket of his jacket a small journal. The cover was made of dark rich leather. He thumbed through the pages with his leather gloved hand. Since the invention of the Personal Digital Self device or PDS few would type messages or notes let alone hand write. The journal had all sorts of mysterious charts and tables. Many of the letters written in it were ancient and strange. Pictures of continents and oceans could be seen. And what looked like ocean currents. Then there was a complete replica of the design that was seen on Hanno's chest. It was a circle with similar characters on the inner edges of the circle like numbers on a clock. There was a clear set of writings underneath the characters. The image was detailed and full of symbols. He arrived at a page that had a hand drawn picture of

Hanno riding a wave on the ocean with the Salty Tallywhacker in the background.

The top read a short line, "He continues to find peace in the sea."
The man then retrieved from under his jacket a pen device. When he wrote the pen hovered several centimeters above the page and the ink more like burned into the paper rather than marked. Again strange characters and shapes formed on the page. Then with unique strokes the man drew the scene of Hanno swimming in the race.

CHAPTER 3:
THE SALTY
TALLYWHACKER

Hanno barely even bothered getting dressed. He had thrown on his button down beach shirt without buttoning it. He cleared the locker room and was up on the quad heading toward the train to the ground. As he walked he became overwhelmed with an itch. His privates and his inner thighs had become inflamed with a rash from the chlorine in the pool. He was trying to scratch it without using his hands. He walked funny as he tried to use his legs rubbing together to itch. He couldn't take it no more. He ducked behind a building and scratch like a crazy man. Then slightly pulled out his trunks and his legs were bright red with bumps. The closer he got to the train stop the more the rash grew. Now his arms were itchy. Then his neck. Then all of his lower legs. He turned bright red with bumps everywhere. He jumped on a train just before the door closed. He made his way to the back to find an empty train car so he could scratch. As the train pulled out Moon was right behind him and just missed his train.

"Hanno?" She said to herself with worry.
Moon jumped on the next train. The ride from Midway to the ground was the worse he had ever experienced. The uncomfortable constant itchiness. And inching the rash made it even worse. His uncomfortableness and itchiness blinded out the beautiful view. Moon arrived to the ground and was looking everywhere for Hanno. The Port was very busy and there were people everywhere. She slowly made her way out of the main area and found herself along the river front walkway. She saw a portion of his surfer shorts sticking out of a corner of a small covered bench. She rounded the corner and then she was right in front of him. He was bent over inching his thighs vigorously. And when he saw her, he froze in that position.

"I can explain."

She lightly chuckled, "I bet."

Instantly he turned around and stood up and then said, "Scratch my back please."
She moved toward him and did not think her first time she would touch him would be like this. She started out slow.

He said, "Oooooh you have nails. Harder."
She smiled strangely and then started scratching harder. He moved and squirmed with her hands. Her smile grew as she had fun with it. It was odd

and intimate in equal portions.

He turned and they locked eyes. He was itching his chest.

"I don't know what happened. I think I am having an allergic reaction."

She grabbed his arm and lifted his swim shirt, "OMG, you have a rash everywhere."

Then she pulled down the collar and looked closer at his neck. A portion of his mark could be seen and he shirked back a little.

"I think I'm allergic to the pool." He said naively.

"Have you never gone swimming before?"

"Well of course I swim every day in the ocean."

"No I mean have you never gone swimming in a pool."

He paused like he wasn't sure, "Well I don't know."

She asked, "What do you mean you don't know?"

Another inching spasm started hitting him and he chased the inch from his neck to his toes. He sat straight down on the ground and was inching the bottom of his feet.

"I've never seen a rash on the bottom of person's feet."

Several of the pedestrians looked at the two of them.

"Are you breathing ok? I've heard that an allergic reaction can cause your neck to swell and make it hard to breath."

He paused from scratching and took in a deep breath.

   "I think so."

Then back to scratching this time trying to scratch his back.

      She just said, "Come on I have an idea."

She helped him up but then led him by the hand. She led him to the end of the riverfront dock. The Wilmington Port not only had trains coming and going but it also had a series of boats. Many parts of the open ocean had become too hazardous to navigate. When nukes and global weapons were used the sea was changed forever. But the river still had lots of tourist boats coming and going. As they walked along the riverfront there were all sorts of streamline and futuristic looking ships. Many made out of illuminist metals, several which ran or rather hovered on some sort of energy just above the water. One mid-sized ship about thirty feet long slowly came up out of the depths and broke the surface like a small sized submarine. It rose up between several other larger passenger ships. It was all black and long and streamlined. It had two cylinders attached to wings that were on each side that were clearly some sort of jet propulsion. Then there was a narrow pointed front and three large metal fins at the back one going up and two to each side. The center of the ship had a glass top and small antenna. It looked like a streamlined personal underwater ship that could carry a team of six or seven at most. It was slowly following them. Moon then led Hanno down a set of stairs to the riverfront.

"Maybe the saltwater will help."

Hanno still itching, "This is the Cape Fear River it's not the ocean."

Moon then just said, "Come on Hanno this is an estuary, there's lots of salt water mixed in with the fresh."

"Yeah good point."

He took off his swim shirt and would have took of his shorts too if he could. He dove right in and sure enough the salt and natural water started working a miracle. The rash was going away.

There was a soft section of grass that adjoined the riverfront. It slopped steeply as it went down. Hanno after a good swishing and swashing in the river came out and sat down on the grass. Moon joined him. He still had his shirt off and was almost all the way dry. She was running her finger over his neck and chest checking his rash.

"It's almost completely gone."

Her flirtatious touch did not go unnoticed. He leaned in and they kissed softly for a while. It was a first kiss for both of them and the whole air felt electric. Afterwards, she moved her finger from his chest to his tattoo. She traced the characters and symbols. Going from the center to the outside was raised markings that looked like branches or brackets. Different paths of the brackets took you to different symbols. The symbols on the inside of the circle were flat. But on the outermost edge of the design the letters and symbols were raised and more like a brand than a tattoo. The inside writing was barely visible. And the fonts grew the closer you got to the edge. Then within the center the letters and shapes when looked at an angle appeared to form a completely other design. All of the words and letters were foreign and strange. At the very center of the design was a single picture. The picture was dense and very detailed. She got closer and it looked like a series of atoms or no maybe planets. With bands, rings and clusters of bright looking stars in blue, purple, yellow, and orange set in a sea of blue. Way too dense and detailed to see with the naked eye. He became self-conscious and took her hand in his.

From the middle of the river too far to be seen by the young couple was the all black sub vessel. It floated with only a portion of its structure above water. Following the antenna from above the surface down into the ship we see inside the passenger compartment. Inside looked more like the inside of a super expensive luxury vessel. As soon as we enter the inside it is clear that we are inside a vessel that is full of water. The occupants there are strange but humanoid looking. They clearly are at home in the water. When we see from their perspective the water filled chamber is full of light and they can communicate and it sounds no different when humans communicate in the air filled world above. There was a control section where four individuals sat. Two facing the front of the vessel as pilot and co-pilot. One facing the side working communications. And one facing the opposite direction of the pilots. The antenna fed into his station. As the signal came into the controls there was an attached device that came up out of the controls which had a metallic circle. The circle energized the water and created a video image out of the water in the middle of the circle that showed Hanno and Moon sitting on the slope. As they talked the sounds vibrated and played back like a high depth water screen. The operator up close had deep blue green skin and pointed ears. He was talking to someone in the back of the ship.

"The Rajah appears to have found himself a mate."

A deep dark voice answered from somewhere unseen, "Enough chatter."

The operator only answered, "Yes sir."
As the crew observed from their vessel they were watching Hanno and Moon.

Hanno now holding Moon's hand in his lap said, "The reason I didn't remember if I had ever swam in a pool is because I don't remember my past."

"What do you mean?"

"All I know is that I showed up as a child on the beach and almost died from a shipwreck."

"Oh my, really how long ago was that?"

"Three years now."

The scene changes to a violent storm. Waves are crashing on the beach and also on the pier. From the sky huge surges of ocean can be seen stretching far into the grounder inland. After the war major changes in the earth's plate technology had been causing numerous tsunamis. And today's storm was no different. Roads and low lands for miles into the grounders land under the sky city were being rushed with flooding water. A huge burst of sea air blew open a port hole window. Water blew through the opening and splashed down on the face of Seth Vandergriff. Above the Salty Tallywhacker was a lighthouse. The Vandergriffs had lived there for many generations. Seth fought to close the window. Then he quickly got dressed and wound his way down the stairs of the lighthouse. Another explosive burst in a lower window. Seth rushed outside and pushed closed and re-hooked the edge that came loose. He then stopped and looked out into the storm. The wind blasts and sea swell were the size of a category five hurricane. But small potatoes to what the area had experienced since the war. It was always rumored that it was the nuclear bomb that missed Hawaii but hit the pacific that set the plates in motion. Seth looked out in the ocean with a mariners resolve. Still at awe of the power of God's creation. Then he thought he saw a small sea creature on the beach just outside of his pier. At first it looked like a mammal but then something else, but the rain was falling sideways and he could not see clearly. Then he saw it clearly it was a boy.

"They think I was thirteen but I really don't know how old I am."

At that moment looking into his eyes Moon did think he looked much older.

"I don't know who my parents are. I don't know where I was born."

He continued to explain, "Mr. Vandergriff found me with only a torn shirt and a pair of underwear. And I had this."

He pointed to the design on his chest. Along the inner circle between the outer characters and the inner branches was as single name written, "Hanno."

Inside the sub, the water screen zoomed in on the design and locked it and then moved it to a file.

The controller spoke out, "We have the design."

From the back of the sub we now see the hidden figure he was talking to. The area looked like the backseat of a luxurious limo with deep leather seats. The figure was in a long dark cloak holding a glass of some substance. As he drank his cloak appears more like a floating portion of his skin then clothing. He had a black hood that floated in the water in the sub. It was dark and heavy and it covered completely his whole head. Then the hood too appeared more like a vestige of his underwater body. It face was dark within the hood. Looking deeper within the hood was a dark red eye that was one eye but also appeared as two eyes. The eyes that Hanno saw in his nightmare on the battle on the ship.

He then commanded, "We have enough. Is the track on his PDS working?"

"Yes Sir."

"Move to the next target."

The mysterious ship sunk back down into the sea. Some time had gone by and Hanno and Moon were back at the port. Hanno and Moon were walking hand in hand. They were heading back up to the trains when suddenly a news alert came over both their PDS's. A video screen came up and a reporter was speaking.

"A family favorite and long term beloved character of Surf Cities Salty Tallywhacker, Seth Vandergriff was killed today."

Hanno's face sunk.

"You were just talking about him."

"I have to go there."

Moon flipped a screen and looked at the time, "But it's almost curfew."

"I don't care I have to go."

"I'll go with you."

Hanno and Moon arrived from the train station. It was already dark. They could see lots of blue and red lights at the pier. There was a huge police response and all of the roads were blocked off. They went down to the sea and approached the store from the beach side. On this end there was a small crowd of locals starting to form. A bright electronic yellow crime scene beam blocked off the crime scene. As they stood with the crowd looking on the scene in the background in the dark sea, the mysterious sub slowly sunk into the ocean off in the distance. Above was a hovering command post that was floating with ease up and to the side of the store. There was a temporary energy staircase that went down to the entrance of the crime scene from the street side. In the sky above the store, were sleek silver and blue drones flying over the scene. On top of the drones where blue lights slowly flashing as they moved and passed over the area. Below each drone was a deep blue beam that was scanning and 3D mapping the scene. Inside the command post several detectives were watching a large screen as the mapping results fed into the command post. Two medium sized drones where carrying a body bag and then loaded it up into floating vehicle that only had a cargo hold and did not appear to have any driver or passenger areas. On the side it read, "Coroner." Hanno's face fell and Moon reached out and grabbed his hand.

"I'm so sorry Hanno. I had only known Mr. Vandergriff for a short period but he seemed really nice."

"When he found me he tried to adopt me but the Bliss would not let him and entered me into grounders foster care."

Each and every occupant of the coastal area was as strictly controlled as the sky city itself. Since it was considered an extension of the city.

"If it were not for him getting me a work visa and the job at the shop; I might never had been allowed at the beach again."

One of the drones then also was scanning the surrounding crowd for witnesses and suspects. As the drones beam touched down on the civilians below each person's PDS blinked slightly and the data was fed into the command post. The screen would show their name, picture, and other government data associated with each person. When it got to Hanno the computer stopped and a small red flag appeared.

The Bliss's AI computer spoke out in an electronic accent, "Hanno Wilson, sixteen year old, known associate of the deceased and employee of the Salty Tallywhacker."

Hearing the computer AI say the goofy store name caused a couple of younger detectives to laugh and mock it.

In robot voice, "Employee of the Salty Tallywhacker."

A tall lean older detective dressed in a black suit with tails and hat like the mysterious man at the swim meet, stepped from the other room. He seemed like he was sky bred and raised. His suit and style all spoke of him having a much higher social standing then what was usual for police work.

"You two shut up."

The computer continued, "Hanno Wilson

has a current watch out order as a foster care runaway."

Now seeing the detective he was a black man in his late thirties. He swiped the screen downward and the file on Hanno sent an icon to his PDS. Then he swiped up and the computer spoke out again.

"Hanno Wilson, pick up order alert. All officers, person of interest."
The message was sent to all the officers in the area. An officer standing at the beach side line PDS blinked and vibrated and then he touched his ear to hear the message for him only. The crowd could not hear it but Hanno was close enough to see his face icon on the officer's wrist right when he turned to start scanning the crowd. Hanno quickly turned away. Grabbing Moon's hand.

"Come on we got to go."
The drone above then locked on him too. It turned on a flood light and they were pinpointed and illuminated in the dark area on this side of the beach. The officer closest saw them illuminated and starting to run in their direction. His patrol uniform better resembled a superheroes outfit. He was fit and muscular and had all sorts of belts and bans on his body with more tools and weapons than batman. He lifted his hand and out of his forearm launched a flying missile weapon of some sort. It locked into Hanno's signal and was tracking and following him as Hanno and Moon dodged and ran through the crowd. It was

only several feet behind them as they ran toward the sea. When it was only feet away Hanno instinctually grabbed Moon and they both ducked behind a large rock that was embedded in the sand near the shore break. A man that they had just ran around was now in the line of the missile and the arsenal deployed an electronic micro net. The net surrounded him and shocked him to the ground into submission. Just then a great earthquake struck the area just off shore. All who were on the beach felt it and many fell to the ground. This was a regular occurrence and most of the officers quickly made their way back to their vehicles and launched and elevated to a safe distance above. Two of the officer's, like hunting dogs were locked on Hanno and were still in pursuit. Civilians ran in all directions. Those from New Atlanta got on their trains and disappeared to the safety in the sky. The locals ran and then climbed on any structure that had several stories. Hanno and Moon ran toward the sea. Off in the distant a huge twenty five foot tsunami formed and started heading their way.

From the ship's pilot in the command center, "Captain Denton, permission to evade."
The black male now known as Captain Denton just stood watching the chase on the screen. The Pilot asked again, "Captain Permission to evade."
Denton moved from the command room to the door. He grabbed a handlebar at the entrance.

"Ok permission granted."

The lights of the command vessel dimmed and the screen turned off. The electronic stairs disappeared and the ship rose away from the strike zone. Denton watched from the open door as Hanno and Moon jumped into the sea right as the wave impacted the beach. The huge wave kept going and pushed inland several miles. A number of civilians and the two cops disappeared under the surge of the water.

Under water we first see from Moon's perspective. It is dark and she is being flipped and tossed by the wave. The only thing guiding her is Hanno as he holds tight to her hand. From Hanno's view the underwater world is bright and beautiful. We see his eyes change and adjust. There are innumerable layers of color and light. Deep green sea plants, bright blue creatures, then a sea turtle swam by and looked right at him. The power of the wave had passed so they surfaced. Moon gasped for air. In the air above several of the drones were still following and searching for them. When one came close they both ducked underwater. Again the view from Moon was dark and dreary. But Hanno saw her and she was wearing a beautiful white sleeveless dress. The dress flowed in the water like a royal gown. The drone was right over head. She struggled to go to the surface. He held both her hands. Then from somewhere within him near where the design on his chest was, the design started to light up with blue energy. The energy then flowed from him and surrounded her. The ocean instantly changed and opened up to her. She now could see like he could. There was the most beautiful school of dolphins that were there the whole time but until that moment she could not see them. There was a great shark off in the distance and a crop of beautiful floating flower hat jelly fish with their bright yellow body and long yellow and purple tentacles.

"What happened I can see?"

He smiled.

"Wait, I can breathe."

She then also realized that she could talk under water too. And it wasn't garbled like before. Her words were as clear as they were above.

He just said, "I know."

"How are you doing this what is happening?"

"I don't know I've always been able to."

As she looked around at all of the undersea wonders her gaze then moved to him. He had let go of her and they were both just floating fifty or so feet below the surface. His hair was alive in the ocean. It wasn't the furry mess as it was above; but very alive and pure looking. His shirt had come open and his body had changed too. His skinny and long body was now lean hard muscle. His arms were also thicker with strong biceps and triceps. Suddenly a blue with black striped tentacle swam within her view past his upper body. She was startled but then followed it down and it was coming from him. Below from somewhere near his legs it came out of him. Out of his surfer shorts were eight thick and muscular blue tentacles with black tiger stipes that wrapped around each tentacle. He was swimming and floating. When he saw her looking below his waist he looked down and noticed them too and then like a man caught naked, he moved quickly and the tentacles disappeared. She then saw his legs and he swam to the surface. Once at the surface they were still close and he was incredibly embarrassed.

"What are you?" She asked with amazement.

When she saw his embarrassment instead of asking more question she just swam to him and grabbed him and gave him a big kiss.

"Ok ok, let's swim to shore."

He was still a little embarrassed but also a little confused himself.

CHAPTER 4:
REVELATIONS,
PUZZLES,
AND CLUES

The tidal wave had cleared the crime scene. The detectives felt satisfied they searched everything that was worth searching. They were already starting to form opinions that it was some dirty grounder that robbed and killed Vandergriff. And several thought that grounder in question was Hanno. They would eventually send salvage drones to attempt to find his body within the wreckage of the latest disaster. The Salty Tallywhacker was surprisingly unaffected. It was up on thirty foot piles above the wave's impact. The pier and the store were made out of very durable polythermal protoplasts. A new form of 3-d printed construction material made to look authentic like natural wood, but much stronger and durable. They approached the electronic yellow crime scene beam and it was still illuminated and surrounding the property. A single hovering drone almost fifty feet up was at the front of the property and the source of the scene sealing. Hanno attempted to duck under the yellow line and hit his face and arm against an invisible shield. The shield came to life and made a bubble of energy at the impact site. Hanno fell to the sandy ground and Moon crotched at his side. The drone as if it felt the impact turned slightly and scanned the area. But they were too far away. Then the drone resumed its position. Scenes like these must have small intrusion attempts by birds, rats, and crabs on a regular basis so Hanno's attempted breach was quickly dismissed. Hanno stood and was looking at the location of the force field. They both observed it and studied it. A slight energy vibration could be seen up close.

"It goes pretty high, I can't see the top."

Moon was next to him and then asked, "Um are we going to talk about what just happened?"

Hanno looked at her apologetically and then back to the shield, "Maybe later, I got to get inside."

She then said, "Ok I mean it's ok, after all I love sea creatures."
She said in her nerdy class room voice.

"Nice, can we concentrate."

"Sure." Then she added, "What about under? Maybe we can dig a big hole in the sand."

"That's a good idea but how deep?"

Then Hanno noticed the pier, "The end of

the pier is pretty deep. I have an idea come on."
To say Moon had always loved the ocean was an understatement. When she was seven her family volunteered to watch sea turtle nests and then helped the baby sea turtles find their way to the sea. From ages ten to fifteen she had become the secretary of the ocean green keepers association. It was an environmental group focused on trying to keep the ocean's clean. When the sky city first launched and the occupants filled it up. The city municipality would just dump the cities brown water down on the ground below the city. Of course this made its way to the ocean. With her organizations lobbying she was able to get them to build the cities first water recycling plant. Although then the grounders had no water falling on them at all.

Hanno stepped into the sea and was about to just start swimming.

Then he stopped and turned to her. "I'm not a sea creature. But I'm not human either."
Looking to her for support.

And she gave it with a huge smile, "I know. I like you Hanno whatever you are."
His shirt buttons had broken and his design was showing. She now saw something in the design she hadn't noticed before.

"Come on."
He reached out to her and she gave him her hand. They swam together along the yellow crime scene shield that extended out to the end

of the pier. He had his arm around her back and was swimming with ease under the water like an underwater jet ski pushing them both forward. When they arrived at the end of the pier he took her underwater. He imparted to her some of his energy again and this time she swam stronger and better than she ever had. Her dress flowed with the water and her hair too. When he looked at her, he was amazed how beautiful she was. She looked different from his underwater eyes. Her long legs kicking under her short dress. They both swam down deep. But the pressure seemed no different than when they were only few feet below the surface. He was filling or sensing the edge of the shield as he went down. The shield was also more visible underwater and they found a spot about hundred feet down where it stopped. The view at the edge of the deep was so breath taking. It was like looking down from atop of a mountain. They paused as she was beside herself at the view. Then they both swam under the shield.

"Good thing we didn't dig in the sand."

She laughed, "Right."

Then up back to the surface. She was so excited to be swimming, breathing, and seeing underwater. Since she was a little girl she had wanted to be a mermaid. Now with Hanno she practically was. They came up under the pier and on the other side of the yellow line. Slowly they swam up to the beach at the bottom of the pier. It was darker now and the wave that had passed had caused a black out to the region. Anyone left alive, had made their way inland so the whole coastal city was vacant. They went up to the back door. Hanno retrieved a key from around his neck attached to a unique necklace. The necklace was similar in design to his chest markings.

"What are you hopping to find?"

"Seth told me a month ago that he had something for me. And that he was going to give it to me on my birthday."

"Birthday, when's that?"

"Today, August 21st. Well not birthday more like anniversary of when I washed ashore."

They made their way through the store. First they checked the store. Nothing. Then the office and store room in the back. Still nothing. Then at the back of the store near the office was the stairs up to the lighthouse. They made it round and round to the midway point when Moon heard something.

"What was that?"

"It sounded like the front door."

Then they could hear that someone was in the store below them. Hanno just put his finger to his lips and they slowly kept climbing. They got to the top of the light house. It was cozy like a second office with a 360 degree view. The moon was out and there was some natural light shining in. They heard a loud thud. It sounded like someone had pushed over a bookshelf in the office below. Over Hanno's shoulder through the window the mysterious sub had reappeared and was floating just off the coast and also at the end of the pier. Hanno and Moon had not noticed it and kept searching. Under the desk they found a medium sized trunk. It had a latch and the latch had a lock. Moon found it first and looked at the lock.

"It has five tumblers, each tumbler has thirteen letters A to Z."

She was thumbing through the letters and Hanno kept looking down the stairs. Then someone came in the stairwell and swept the stairs with light. Hanno jumped back from the opening.

"Someone's here." He whispered with freight.

Below one of the green lizard skinned crew mates of the slick futuristic sub was moving in the dark. He had on a dark black armored uniform with red markings. His head was bald with hard green scales. His ears were small and almost non-existent pushed up against his head like a fish. In his hand was some sort of energy weapon. Then several more of the green crew members came into sight. One had a similar weapon with a light attached. The two with weapons were searching and sweeping the area looking for Hanno and Moon. The other two were searching the shop. Hanno saw the lights moving in the shop below. He started looking around for a weapon. In the background Moon was working the lock puzzle.

"Salty S.A.L.T.Y?"

She tried it. The lock wouldn't budge. Hanno grabbed a large book off the shelf. But then one of the ends came off and a bunch of notes fell to the ground.

"Ocean O.C.E.A.N.?"

One of the green men were searching the front of the store. He was near the register and found a small bottle of whiskey. He opened it and took a deep pull. Behind him coming into view was the man that was at the swim tryouts with the dark suit and dark hat. He slowly pulled from his back under, the tails of his suit, two thin swords. The swords were too long to be considered knifes but too short to really look like swords. Then as if the creature sensed something behind him, he quickly turned and then attempted to pull his own knife. The dark man made a very quick step then a slash and a jab. The green man dropped to the ground. The smash sound caught the others attention. The leader had made it to the back of the store at the base of the winding stairs. When he heard the thud, he stopped going up the stairs and turned to head to the front. The other two came right at the man. One in front pulled a long thick knife. He moved with training and style toward the man in black. But the man was too quick and highly trained with his two knife swords. He double jumped and seemed to fly through the air. He dodged the enemy's knife and sliced his neck but then was suddenly behind him and finished him from behind. Even as he started to move, the third green creature started shooting with his weapon. The sound was deep and low and almost inaudible. But the light from the weapon struck like lightning. Then just as thunder often arrives after lightening the sound of the weapon exploded loudly only seconds after its light. The man moved swiftly around the energy bolts.

Crack

The front counter exploded.

Crack, crack,

The bolts struck his own comrade as the man in black had already pulled his sword. He was now moving on the third. Two more ducks and dodges and he was on top of him. Step, slice, the creature's weapon and hand were removed. The blade was so sharp it appeared to separate the flesh and metal more than cut. Then as his first blade had not even finished its path the blade in his other hand landed into the creature's chest. Green substance oozed out.

Hanno hearing the fight now grabbed a large beer mug with the store's name on it. When he lifted it and position it for an attack, beer spilled on him.

"Eh gross."

He quickly put it down.

Moon was still working on the lock, "Beach B.E.A.C.H.?"

She tried it and the lock didn't move. Hanno found a picture on the corner of the desk. It was of him and Seth standing at the end of the pier. The look on Seth's face was like a proud father.

"Try Hanno."

"Of course, H.A.N.N.O."

The lock clicked open. Moon opened the trunk and right inside on top was the most intricate and decorated short sword. The sheath was decorated with markings and designs similar to Hanno's chest markings. It was dark blue with black designs running the length. He grabbed it and unsheathed it. The handle was blue and black and long and lean. The blade was pitch black thin and sharp with deep blue engravings. The blade length was 17 inches long and the overall sword length was 25 inches. There was a very sharp tip and a small rip saw spine. It looked like a survival knife perfectly made for underwater. It was perfectly balanced too. When Hanno grabbed it he had a flash of a memory of shoving the knife into a back pack just before he was blown from the ship.

As the man in black moved to the back of the store the leader of the green creature squad slowly moved away into the shadows. The man in black had lost his fedora hat with the thin black veil that hid his neck and portions of his face. As he came into the light that was coming in the window from the moon his face was fully seen. He was a man in his fifties. In the moonlight he had a slight bluish tint to his skin. His ears were sharp and pointed. And on the back of his neck leading down to his back were long deep blue markings. Similar in style and design as Hanno's. The moon light seemed to make the markings glow and energize them. He looked up the winding stairs and saw

Hanno standing at the top of the stairs. Hanno was not aware that the light shown brighter into the lighthouse and was casting light on him making him more visible to the man below. But still hiding the man from Hanno's sight.

Now as the man in black relaxed his fighting stance, we can see he has the same exact short swords as Hanno had just found. The man put the swords away under his tails into the back sheaths. The man looked around and saw the three green creature's bodies. From an inside pocket he pulled three small disc's. They had a flat hard surface on one side and a clear glass on the other. The discs were about the size of a silver dollar. He quickly and artfully through the discs at the three dead creatures like a man dealing poker cards. As each disc landed on the chest or back of the dead creature, the disc first vibrated and then in an instant sucked in the whole of the creature into the disc. There was very little sound other than a quick whoosh for each. Picking up the discs he then moved cautious out the back door and down to the beach under the pier. The man paused and looked out into the water. There was as slight movement of water over the surface. We see the man's eyes change, similar to how Hanno's eyes changed underwater. And he can now see deep under water the fourth green creature swimming to his sub. Suddenly behind him Hanno and Moon were coming out the back door. They were being way too loud but thought they were being sneaky.

As soon as they came out the door they were carrying the trunk between the two of them. The man then adjusted his body and suit and became completely camouflaged into the side of the shop, including his shoes appearing as sand. Hanno and Moon walked by him and then down to the water. The man could see that the sub was moving out to sea and felt they were safe.

Hanno and Moon had wrapped the trunk in thick shipping plastic that Mr. Vandergriff used to send t-shirts in the mail. Then vacuum sealed it with a handheld device. This time because of the buoyancy of the trunk Hanno had to fully release his muscular tentacles. His tentacles pushed them forward. In addition to the tentacles there was a powerful natural jet stream seen coming from below and underneath his body. The power of the tentacles and the jet made it easy work moving the air sealed trunk down one hundred feet and back up again. Once back on the beach on the other side of the yellow line carrying the trunk wasn't too bad for the two of them. Each had ahold of a handle at the end and were walking on the beach. Both were shoeless, wet and exhausted.

"Where to aqua man?" She said to him with a smile.

"Not funny, I prefer Submariner."

They were exhausted and stopped and sat down at the train stop. He leaned over and they exchanged a sweet kiss. The train arrived and stopped in front of them.

"How about my place?" She said temptingly looking up to the floating city.

He looked up too with hope. As they passed through the door a small scanner at the entrance tagged his PDS. The power went out and a small alarm went off. But nothing tagged her. He stepped back and started moving away from her. She was on the train with the trunk.

"Meet me at school."

"But your tagged how will you get there?"

"I'm not sure but I have an idea."

As he got farther away, the train started back up and started pulling away. Moon was alone on the train with one hand up against the glass.

"I think I love you my merman."

He ran off into the darkness as security drones swamped the area of the train station.

CHAPTER 5:
THE ORDER OF
THE BLISS

Moon's train didn't just stop at the city center train stop up in New Atlanta. Her PDS swipe gave her access to her own train which passed the city center and continued up and into the heart of the city. Trains and flying vehicles were everywhere even at this late hour. She had swiped her PDS upon entry and her small individual car within the train actually separated from the rest of the train and now followed its own path not supported by any structure. Up into the heights of the city her car flew arriving at floating luxury complex that floated above but was a part of the floating city. There was two doormen on the landing platform that greeted her.

"Good evening Ms. Cadel, can we help you with your case?"

Sliding her foot in front of it in an instinctual way, "No I've got it."

Then she comically struggled lugging it onto the

elevator. She then went even farther up to a house halfway up the building. Out of the elevator was gardens and a beautiful fountain of water that was fed from two sides of the room. The garden's ceiling was made of the same semi-visible metal and was open to the night sky. The stars shone brightly as she pulled walking backward the trunk to her room which was a sphere shaped room off the garden. As she passed through the doorframe she dropped the trunk. The sound went out through the whole house. A lone figure at the other end of the gardens poked his head out of an office.

"Moon is that you?"

"Yes Daddy."

"What are you doing so late?"

"A homework project daddy."

The man entered back into his study. In this room was a long dark Purple suit hanging on a decorative suit stand. It was similar to the one the man in black wore. The suits seemed almost retro style like some early British era suit with collar, tails, and all. But the material was different. More smooth and elegant. On the collar of the suit was an even deeper purple emblem that had one thin purple line. Zooming in on the emblem suddenly the scene has advanced into the next day. Moon's father, Lord Cadel, stepped out of very stylish flying transport ship. He moved with his security team and entered the building. The huge new bright building was designed with a mixture of light purple marble and some other material that shone and was emitting the same energy that ran, lifted and filled the glorious floating city. The building was a social and judicial landmark at the center of the massive city. It floated hundreds of feet above the cities ground level. Chiseled across the decorative entrance was *The House of the Honorable Bliss of Council.* Or known more commonly as the headquarters of *The Bliss.* The center court yard was open in the middle of the building to all thirteen floors. On each side were offices and landings that had balconies that looked out into the entrance court yard below. Lord Cadel arrived on the seventh floor and passed through a number of security check points. Security for the Bliss were one and the same as the security police force that had investigated the death of Seth Vandergriff.

Lord Cadel was stopped at the entrance suite by several of his advisors.

"Sir could we get a couple quick seconds?"

"Yes, yes, go ahead."

"There was a report of a small prayer meeting in the south sector. When B units arrived there was in fact an in home Christian church."

B units stood for The Bliss Codes and Orders enforcement branch. It covered everything from, Bliss rules enforcement to religious eradication. Just prior to the big war there was enormous political polarization, extreme lefts and extreme rights. Those on the right espoused themselves to toxic and violent religious extremism. After the war religion in any form was marked as illegal and against the purpose and goals of true science. There was such a revulsion toward the politicized religion that well-meaning genuine Christians were outlawed too.

Lord Cadel looking at the report projected by the PDS, "In new castle, Christians?"

"Yes sir, a former contractor for the Bliss."

"Standard response. Burn all print and digital material. Pull all rights and property. Relocation to the Ground."

"Yes sir right away."

Lord Cadel entered a command center that was circular in shape. It was elevated and also floating up and a part of the main building. All of the structures in the city, although often separated and semi-visible, were somehow connected by a unique glow and energy just beyond the visible spectrum. The Command Center look out through semi-visible floors and walls down onto the city below but it also had surrounding virtual screens that monitored everything; the movement of trains and vehicles, the movement of pedestrians, surveillance cameras from all over the floating city, surveillance from areas on the ground along the edges of the city, and feeds from individuals PDS's. Cadel stood at the back of the room. The room was full of analysts and operatives. There was a watch commander at the center of the room. When the senior detective arrived, Cadel looked at him like that was what he was waiting for.

Cadel spoke out, "Commander give me an analyst, Jenson and yourself. All others leave the room."

The room emptied out and the detective and Cadel approached the commander at the center.

"Show me last night."

The analyst brought up numerous videos from the Vandergriff crime scene. They watched Vandergriff close his store. They saw customers leave. Then video black out. Then arrival of the security force. Then lastly the alert on Hanno and the drones focusing on him. Video black out again. The cameras didn't come back up until one caught Hanno running off into the night away from the train station. No video of Moon and no video of the suspects.

Cadel asked, "Detective Denton what do you think happen?"

Detective Ezekiel Denton was not born in New Atlanta. He was born a grounder. He worked the train security detail in Wilmington and found success after success until he was upgraded to citizen. It was rare and everyone knew it. He was grounder born but learned the sky playing field quickly. He knew he was being used by them, but he was using them as well.

Denton then answered, "Everything points to the kid but my gut is telling me something else is going on."

The commander spoke over him, "Surf City

has been seeing a great number of video bugs lately. I've got a crew scheduled to go check our systems. But my guess is the grounders are sabotaging them."

Cadel watched the feeds, "Bring up feed 127 again."
It was the feed that showed Hanno as he turns toward a really good camera on the outside of the train station. The video shows his shirt flip open and his chest markings are visible.

Cadel to the operator, "Freeze image. It couldn't be."
Cadel storms out leaving everyone surprised. Denton looked at the image closely. The commander was distracted on the video failures. Denton moved closer to the analyst.

Then the analyst started nerding out, "Looks elven in design. When I was in school we learned about all the elven influences in math and physics. Most of our technology comes from those early years when they helped us after the war. Well you know before we ruled them as being 'Outside of the Bliss."
He used air quotes but at some point Denton stopped listening and looked even closer. He used his hands to control the screen and opened up and zoomed in. He too recognized the design as elfish.

The analyst continued, "The Lua elves were first documented by the inhabitants of Sao Miguel Island. Of course Lua in Portuguese means Luna or Moon. Some stories say they were found in a cave.

Others that they washed up on the shore. They actually are not from the Moon at all. They were only called that because their skin glowed brighter at night under the Moon. Really don't know why. They seemed more like Water Elves if you ask me. Well with..."

Denton interrupted, "Jenson can you send this video to my drive?"

Jenson continued as he worked, "Many conspiracy theories believe that they are actually still living amongst us to this day just under cover you know. There is a legend that if you find the doorway into their dimension, that it is lined with Trachanjan Gold. A literally pot at the end of the rainbow. The Mysterious legendary treasure."

Denton frustrated, "I know about the legend of the Trachanjan treasure. It's a myth."

The analyst more talking to himself, "Myth or not would love to find it."

Denton stepped out on a balcony of the command center. He was facing the ocean and it looked off in the distance.

The flying cities of planet earth were massive. There were three in the America's, one in over the Mediterranean Sea, and one in Asia near the Mongolia/China border. All of them could be seen from space. Most of the continents below had become destroyed by radiation, flooding, or worse, and many areas occupied by savages. The ground below New Atlanta was about the same as the rest. The floating city touched eight state lines but actually only covered three, Georgia, South Carolina, and North Carolina. The next closest floating City was over the great lakes. And the last one was over Brazil. New Atlanta ran parallel to the Atlantic coast line. It was oblong and longer than it was across. It aligned with the coast on one side and the mountains on the other. But the land under the city had turned back to sand. It was desolate and almost always dark. Whatever the bombs and war had not devastated the blocking of the sun by the massive city structure completed. Most of the grounders lived on the edges of the cities. There was trading and resources there, but also more natural resources and that could growth. The tectonic plates had been affected by the war too. The earth's surface was unstable. There were constant earthquakes and Tsunami's. The oceans were so unpredictable and violent no ships dare try to sail them. Fortunately the new technology opened up the world of flying cargo ships which also allowed trading and travel between these massive cities.

For five days in a row Moon showed up at school with no sight of Hanno. She had hid the trunk in her room. Her thought was she would meet up with Hanno and somehow sneak him into the city. Of course his security flag would make this impossible. On day five she even went down to the beach after school. She asked around with some of the grounders that worked at the restaurants and stores near the surf shop. But no sign.

A huge flying cargo tanker moved out from the southern edge of New Atlanta heading out over the Atlantic Ocean. The next grounder train stop wasn't until you got to Charleston. There were grounder settlements in and around both Wilmington and Charleston. But somewhere about half way between the two near what used to be North Myrtle beach, Hanno got off the train and started heading on foot under the city. The deeper you got under the city the more dangerous it was. This was exactly where Hanno was going. Although many of the ground structures were gone, surprisingly many roads remained. He had hitched a ride with a modern day steam punker named Joe. Joe had converted his motorhome into a steam powered vehicle. All he needed for fuel was wood, coal, or anything flammable and he was mobile.

Hanno looking out the window, "So your def. heading to Oasis?"

Joe looked at him a little paranoid. He was wearing a pair of welding goggles with clear lens because his Motorhome had no front windshield.

"Never been huh?"

"No first time I guess."

Joe looked at his wrist, "Well your going have to ditch the tech."

Hanno looked down at his wrist, at his PDS.

"Yeah I know. I have everything on this. My schoolwork, my caseworker's number, man even my girlfriend's number."

"Well you can kiss that all good bye."

Hanno looking at the strange dirty man, "Is it true what they say?"

"What?"

"You know, that there are cannibals under the city?"

"Well maybe some of them." Joe said with a slight grin.

"That's why I have ol faithful here."
He patted a sawed off double barrel shotgun strapped to his side.

"Who or what are you looking for anyways. Not often I find hitchhikers this far south."
Hanno looked out on the vast desert which used to be lush loblolly and pine forests. He could not imagine ever being so far from the sea.

"Honestly I'm looking for answers?"

Joe's motorhome with the huge center steam pipe chugged its way under the massive city. It was like having an ever present dark moon floating right over your head. Of course it was several thousand feet above but the massive size made it seem closer. Under the city was like a never ending desert at night. The whole east coast had been devastated first by nuclear war. Atlanta, Charlotte, DC, and New York or rather any city worth anything was gone. Nothing was left of the cities but radiation and devastation. Even the nation's highway system had been destroyed. But smugglers like Joe knew the side roads and dirt paths that connected to whatever roads were left. And if that didn't work, he would sometimes just drive on the open deserted, empty land. He had huge push bars on the front and busting through a few fences or pushing a few broke down cars didn't even slow him down. Off in the distance you could see the Former Oasis Great Recovery Center or OGRC. It stood like a beacon in the desert wilderness. The closer they got, the bigger it grew. Of course there were all sorts of tribal settlements throughout the grounders world. But Oasis was one of the most successful. Shortly after New Atlanta launched, the OGRC was created. They made a huge dome stadium out of steel and glass. It was built somewhere between what used to be Dillon South Carolina and Lumberton North Carolina. Its location was chosen because of its proximity to the center of the city above. But also far away from any radiated former major cities. It was fed with water by the Great Pee Dee River system and was self-sufficient. It was designed as a rescue operation center for survivors and refugees. Those that arrived were given food, shelter, water and medical care. Then they would evaluate each for citizenship into the city above. A tower structure was built near the dome. It rose up thousands of feet to the bottom of the city. The city floated above it but was connected to it. The city did not rest on the tower but was attached to it. If the tower fell it would have no effect on the city above. When The Bliss took over they debated about destroying the tower. But then just flooded it. Oasis was on its own. Over time Oasis turned into a massive hub for illegal trade and a haven for all sorts of dangerous grounders. On the North side of the dome was remnants of a bizarre tourist attraction named South of the Border. Very few realized that the family owned quiche tourist spot was owned by a family of preppers. They had built elaborate underground shelters and a network of survival caves to outlast the apocalypse. No one knows where they went or if they survived. Several hundred years after New Atlanta abandoned Oasis, a man named John Granger or just Padre, found the bunkers and turned it into his Oasis HQ.

Joe's motorhome pulled up to the massive gate made of steel that surrounded Oasis. A well-armed guard approached. Hanno had forgot about the PDS. He quickly hid his arm and moved his skin cells so that they first turned blue then the PDS that was under his skin looked like it was pushed up until it was laying on top of his arm. Then his arm turned back to normal color. He quickly grabbed it, crushed it with his other hand and threw it out the window.

"Name and purpose?"

Joe answered, "Trader, got lots of sky tech." And he did. In every available space in the motorhome was salvaged tech. Guards check them for PDS's with some sort of wand scanner, then they were waved in.

"What do you know about this Granger character?" Hanno asked.

Joe got nervous, "Why what did he say about me?"

"No no I just need to see him."

"Well don't tell him about me."

They parked and Joe started loading up a floating cart with some of his tech. Hanno got out and stretched his legs. The dome was massive. There was all sorts of ground vehicles parked in huge empty sandy fields all around it. There was a make shift steel wall around the perimeter. It was the strangest mix of new and old tech he had ever seen. They made it past the gates and found their way into the center. In the center were lines and lines of homemade booths, stands, and carts set up for trade. As the two of them made their way, Joe reached and touched the young man's arm.

"Hanno watch yourself around Granger."

CHAPTER 6: A PATH ABOVE AND BELOW

Moon had just gotten home from school. It was a Wednesday and she had to get her homework done and go to a Bliss training class for young adults. When she came in the door and starting passing the gazebo she noticed the fountains were turned off. Instead of the smell of a perfectly synthesized dinner, she found her entire family waiting for her. Her Dad stood still at the opening of his office and was finishing up a conversation with someone unheard on his PDS. In the adjoining living room off the side of the garden was her brother Brody, and her mother. There was also several female detectives from Bliss and Detective Denton.

Lord Cadel on his PDS "ah huh, yeah, at least not until next week."

Her dad looked at her and she felt it to her core.

Her first thought, "They found the trunk."

But then she thought, "They found my

bible."

Brody had a smirk on his face that said, "I told you so."

Her dad hung up, "Moon have a seat."
He motioned to a sitting room that was off the garden and also open to the side veranda. It was open on three sides but also had a view of the whole lower city.

Moon instantly defensive, "Daddy it was a class history project we were…"

Brody blasted, "History I bet that's what you were studying."
She was thinking trunk, but now she wasn't sure what they were talking about.

Her father sat across from her, "Honey lots of us can be moved and find connections with grounders but that's why we are taught by the Bliss to, 'Protect or heart motives and look to the Bliss for guidance."

Moon confused, "Yes Daddy I always try to keep to the pattern as laid out. But aren't we also to show compassion to those less fortunate."

Cadel pushed in, "Tell me about Hanno."

Moon tried to hide her emotions, "Oh he's a friend from my Oceans class. We have a homework project together."

Mrs. Cadel then spoke up, "Homework down at the beach after 2 am? Quit lying and tell us the truth."
Moon saw the writing on the wall. How could she be so stupid? She knew everything was watched.

That her Dad had the 'Eyes of the Bliss.' But she was motivated by curiosity at first but now by love.

"Hanno is a good man."

Her father interrupted her, "He is a grounder! There is no place for you to be mixed up with a grounder."

She pleaded, "Daddy you don't understand."

Her mother from her side said, "Honey is it true you were at a murder scene with him?" Denton cocked his head slightly watching her every move.

Moon started crying, "You don't understand. Hanno didn't do anything. He's ..."

Cadel was quick to pass judgement. He stood and started walking away, "You are suspended from school. You will be forbidden from leaving the city. You are required to undergo recertification."

Denton leaned in slightly trying to get his attention.

Cadel continued, "Oh and you will give Detective Denton a full statement and help with his investigation in any way he requests."

Moon was stone cold devastated. She was frozen in time. The two female detectives were more concerned about politics than they were about security procedures. They kindly and gently made their way closer to Moon. Moon knew what this meant. She would be in the highly restrictive girl's school controlled by the Bliss. She would never see Hanno again.

Brody laughed and Cadel sent him away. Mother walked with her to her room. Denton was standing near the edge of the veranda making some notes to his virtual screen. Mother was talking nonstop as the two female detectives were distracted outside the door.

"Now Moon make sure you pack both school and work clothes. You know how the Bliss believes in discipline through chores. One time when I was a little girl…"

Moon wasn't listening to her at all. She was packing a bag but her mother didn't even noticed when she pulled from her closet the huge trunk and opened it. Inside the trunk was the short sword, a back pack full of all sorts of other items. She put her clothes, the smaller pack and all the items of the trunk into her larger backpack. She swung her pack on her back and walked out the door with her chin up. The two detectives had completely misread her. They started heading for the front door without even paying attention to Moon. Denton saw it first. He noticed a look. A look toward the opening. But then even he got lost in his work. She bolted. She ran right for the ledge of the veranda. She flew by Denton and he lunged for her but it was too late. She hurtled the glass guard rail. Denton, the two detectives, and her mother and father ran to the rail. She was skydiving and the building was so high up that she actually had time to glide and look for a landing zone. She moved in and around smaller buildings. At one point she passed through a corridor that was a vertical walkway between two large office buildings. Then she saw it. She adjusted and glided toward her goal. As she passed under a smaller building she flew through some of the purple energy. The energy that was clearly some sort of energy field that held up the building actually energized her body and slowed her down. The small particles of the field seemed to leave the building and attach to her so that she started to float too. But she was still going pretty fast and then splash. In the cities center was a huge park and at the center of the park was Lake Atlanta. Everyone on the balcony exhaled and thought she was dead for sure. But then she swam to the side and looked back at them. And then disappeared into the city.

Hanno had made it across the trader's gazebo, then pass the food carts. He then made it to the northern side of the dome. There was a huge door that looked like at one time it was made to allow huge flying tanker ships through its opening. But now it was connected to a steel walled corridor that led to the South of the Border section of Oasis. Lots of traders and merchants were allowed to leave the dome and set up here as well. This area was tightly controlled with many more guards. And although it was outside the dome it was still within the perimeter of the perimeter steel wall. On this side of Oasis there were mounted positions with gunners and snipers up on the wall itself. Some looking out into the waste lands. But others down on the corridor and the crowds. Hanno made it all the way to the end. At the end was the old tourist park. Here was where travelers and traders waited to be approved or judged. Hanno found himself in a line. A women in her twenties was dressed with a jeans jacket, jean cutoff shorts, black fishnet stalking's and biker boots. Her hair was jet black and her skin was covered with a thick layer of dirt and sand. She had a pair of dark goggles up on her head and a cleaner part that was under the goggles around her eyes showed how much dirt she had caked on her face.

"What's up buttercup? You as clean as a baby."
She was way too sexual and her advances made him uncomfortable.

He answered, "I have a girlfriend."

She looked around, "Oh great let's get a threesome going later."
He really did look much different. It was like the beach front grounders were stuck between the worlds of the civilized sky people and the wasteland grounders. As the line started to move he moved out of line and away from her. As he rounded a corner something happened to his appearance. It happened without him evening controlling it or knowing how it happened; his skin and clothes changed and was now ruddy and dirty and matched all those around him. He

moved toward the center of the city and sat down near a well. He just watched. There were three lines. One at some sort of supply distribution building that used to sell t-shirts and coffee mugs. Another line that was in front of a building that was built between the legs of Pedro, a large sombrero wearing character. And the longest line went to an open stand that appeared to be some sort of vetting process for approving traders. At the line at Pedro was the heaviest security. There was another twelve foot high wall that adjoined on each side of Pedro's legs. This narrow walled off corridor led fifty feet to a larger building. This building was at the base of the tower to the sky. So when Hanno looked up over Pedro he also then saw the tower.

"That must be wear Granger is?" He said to himself.

"And my way back to Moon."

From a side door a strange little man walked out between two buildings. He was only three foot, seven inches tall but he was thick with natural muscles. He looked as if he was well into his fifties and very healthy looking. He had a prosthetic right leg and was wearing heavy strange boots on both feet. He had no shirt on and was covered in tattoos. He was wearing leather wrist bracelets and had a leather belt across his chest. In the belt was a smoking pipe, a multi-tool, a small leather pouch with writing and drawing utensils, and several blueprints attached to a bag at his waist. His head and beard were completely white and long and wild. On his face was a scar that went from his forehead over his left eye and down into his beard. The area where the scar touched his beard, no facial hair grew. He moved slowly and meticulously from the alley out into the pedestrian flow heading toward the large Pedro statue.

He looked out into the crowd and saw order and math. Over each person was an imaginary line. All the lines met in the sky above their heads. Imaginary numbers and formulas formed and moved with the pedestrians.

Mumbling under his breathe, "five hundred and twenty two divided by forty hectors, plus one hundred guards and administrative staff...fifteen point five per hectare...Way too crowded today." His manner with his hands and his gate made it clear that he was cursed and gifted with being different. He was looking down but very aware of his surroundings. He then looked to the wall and saw a mounted gun. We see from his view the parts of the gun are dissembled and charted like an engineer's blueprints in the sky above the gun.

"Browning M2 .50 Caliber, automatic, recoil operated, air-cooled machine gun. US Army third class taken from the battle at Midway. 84 lbs., 850 rpm, 2,900 feet per second muzzle velocity, max range 6,800 meters. Upon impact to human flesh causing devastating lacerations and crushing of bone and tissue causing severe injury or death."

Near the Pedro entrance a large Asian guard came out of the fortified doors.

"Granger is not seeing anyone today!" he shouted.

The crowd was visibly upset. Shouts of anger and frustration rung out. The woman that Hanno had stood by, yelled out that this was some "Bullshirt!" But she said the other word. The crowd became restless and a small riot started to form. The guards on the wall moved to prepare for it. The crowd started rushing in toward Pedro from all sides. A large crowd from the other line behind Hanno moved in too. Hanno moved through the crowd and found himself on the far right but up against the wall.

The small man with tattoos stopped in his path. The vision of numbers moved and changed with the energy of the riot. Above the crowd were velocities, predictions and impact ratios and when one threw a rock, the man saw a physics problem with angle and velocity and knew where it would hit before it did. Which was right in the head of the large Asian guard. He moved his hands with excitement in front of his body. He didn't see a mob. He saw a moving living organism and all of the math and physics that went with it.

Hanno partly by plan but partly by instinct completely, camouflaged his body and blended in with the wall. His body not only matched the color of the wall but it molded and formed to the steels structure including the rivets, seams, and seals. When he realized no one could see him, he then moved with stealth along the wall. His body smoothly moved completely invisible. No one saw him and no one noticed him. Well almost no one. The small man had moved to the far right and climbed a ladder. He was vibrating with energy as he calculated and formulated everyone's movements and actions. He moved a finger over the crowd as he created the formulas and calculations in his mind. The vision of math above the crowd was spinning up with the energy of the crowd. A strange red line branched off of a group of rioters near the wall. The man followed the line to Hanno. Now his focus zoomed in on Hanno. A new set of formulas and engineering schematics formed over the wall and over Hanno. He moved his hands together even faster. Hanno was pass the crowd, had slipped behind the guards and was at the doors. And just before he entered through the opening; he was splashed with a bucket of very cold water making him visible. Right in front of him was the small man. The whole crowd froze in amazement. Hanno was looking at the man.

He talked in a very loud voice, "Humanoid Cephalopod, Humanoid Cephalopod, Humanalopod."

The guards had turned and now too saw Hanno.

In the quiet the man kept talking, "Cephalopod, most intelligent invertebrates, member of the molluscan class comes from Kephalopodes which in Greek means head-feet,

Chromatophore cells using multiple pigments and iridophores and leucophores that activate and polarize changing and moving light. Most likely from the family of Architeuthidae or Architeuthis Dux. Cautions include, ink sac projections, Neurotoxins, harpooning appendages, and then of course lots and lots of tentacles..." he shuffled his hands in excitement.

Then as if nothing out of the ordinary had happened the man slowed his hands and lowered his head, continued to mumble and walked through the doors.

Hanno was brought in with two guards holding both his arms. They entered into a large warehouse the size of a super hardware store but completely underground. Instead of concrete and aisles it was open and full of soil with crops. The senior guard who was still rubbing his throbbing head pointed to where they were to take him. He was left on a dirt trail along the wall. The guards left and secured the door. There was all manner of crops. He remember seeing a large store of fruit and produce above ground and now realized where it was grown. There was one elevated office with a man in his twenties that looked out the window but then appeared uninterested. Hanno thought maybe it was Granger. There were your normal ground crops like corn, carrots, lettuce, celery, and the like. But then there was fruit too. The ceiling was lined with high-tech solar lights. The lights appeared to actually be built right into the ceiling. It was bright, like a bright sunny day. Hanno and Joe had arrived at Oasis in the afternoon and Hanno now realized what he was witnessing. As the sun must have been setting far above New Atlanta down here in the warehouse, the light was moving toward sunset as well. The solar lights were slowly tracking from East to West and creating the illusion of a sunset. There were a number of workers in the fields. It looked like they were harvesting strawberries. He walked along the wall. Near the middle of the room was a lab that was attached to the warehouse. He stopped in the doorway and looked in. Inside was the small man. He was up on a movable ladder writing formulas on a board. From behind him a unique looking worker slowly walked up to Hanno from a row of corn. The man was in his sixties. He had on jeans and no shirt. He was wearing a large straw hat. He was clean shaven but had thick curly white chest and back hair that stood out in his sun or rather solar light darkened tan. The hair also went out over his arms. He looked in good shape from working in the fields all day.

"So I see you met the mathematician." The man asked Hanno.

Hanno looked back at the man and then back at the small man.

"Why do they call him that?"

"Ask him."

They both entered the lab. The worker sat in a chair and pulled from a small fridge a homemade sports drink. Hanno entered the center of the lab. All around were unique inventions and devices. On one side were three dimensional blueprints of New Atlanta floating over an electronic design board. On the other side was a model of a machine that looked like it might be used for space travel. Hanno was amazed at all he saw.

He naively asked, "Why do they call you the mathematician?"
The man got down off the ladder and approached him.

He shyly answered, "Because I'm good at math duh."

The worker then answered, "Jerry here is not just good at math. He is a living computer."
The small man went over to the design table and started working on something.

The worker then motioned to Hanno, "Want something to drink? I made this lemonade tea that is pretty good."

"Your granger aren't you?"
Hanno took a bottle and thanked him with a nod.

"Yep I'm granger. But the question is who or what are you?"

Hanno quickly just answered, "I'm Hanno and I'm trying to get into New Atlanta to go see my girlfriend."

"Well there are girls all around us what makes this girl so special?"
Hanno thought on that when Jerry walked over with a device in his hand and walked around

Hanno scanning him with the device. Then back at the electronic table a 3-D image of Hanno appeared.

"Jerry seems very interested in you. I wonder why. That takes me back to the question. What are you?"

Hanno saw the image over the device and it had calculations for his many possible configurations and appeared to be analyzing him.

"Well I don't really know. I have some memories. I mean I have lost most of my past in some sort of accident."

The screen then centered in on the scan of his chest markings. The computer took off with all sorts of analysis. It appeared to be going deep into all the symbols and found even smaller prints and designs. It searched artifacts of the past. It brought up and searched sea charts. Then quickly went on to Star charts. The symbols were being analyzed, quantified, and then saved. Jerry got excited as the computer moved quickly he absorbed and consumed the data also.

Then the computer spoke out, "Species unidentified. Origin unidentified. Characters, symbols and designs have some matching with Atlantis in mythology and elven in phenotype. The species has thirty times more chromosomes than human and thirteen more than elven."

Jerry rubbing his hands, "Thirteen times, ahhh hahhh."

Granger got up and put on a light silk shirt,

"Jerry is very excited about you."

Jerry went back and started adding his research to the project with New Atlanta.

Granger came closer and in a spooky way used his finger to slightly open Hanno's shirt to get a closer look at the markings.

Hanno pulled back, "Look I'm looking for a way into the city. I have a lot to offer maybe we could come to an agreement."

Granger smiled and moved to the side towards Jerry. "Oh I think we can work something out."

Granger used an old tech communication device attached to the wall to make a call. Several guards took Hanno to a guest room and locked him in.

Granger then just said, "We'll talk in the morning."

CHAPTER 7:
CACAO WINE

Moon had found herself in an area of New Atlanta she had never been seen before. Up on the luxury and privilege part of the floating condos and office buildings it was literally sunny bright skies every day. But at street level or rather below street level it was different. The clouds of the sky formed right at ground level of the floating city. Thus street level was foggy and cloudy often if not daily. All along the cities edge were massive intakes ducts that sucked in the moisture rich vapors. Enough to provide abundantly for the water needs for New Atlanta but leaving a drought in the wasteland below. Except for the coastal areas of course which were not under rain shadow of the city above. Often the clouds floated up and onto the streets causing a real Scooby Do vibe. Moon had tried to take the train back to the beach but encounter the same shutdown and drone alerts that Hanno experienced. Her name was now on the list too. She narrowly escaped security teams on several occasions. Now she was following tips and clues that led her to the shady lower section of city. Down a long, dark alley was a set of stairs. She stood frozen in time looking down seven steps at a creepy metal door. She heard something behind her. A shadow was following her. Not wanting to go forward but having no other options she slowly descended into the darkness. There was a low light near the door. The door that looked pitch black at the top of the stairs was now dark green. She knocked three times like her source on the street told her to do. Nothing.

She knocked again and then said, "I'm here for the sliced potatoes."
The door opened and a very old women in her nineties with a red sweater and a green scarf over her hair just looked at her. She appeared to be chewing but was just moving her mouth with no teeth in.

"I'm here about the sliced potatoes." Moon said again with hesitation.
Did she follow the right directions? Was she at the right place? The older woman just turned and started walking away leaving the door open. Moon followed her into the small and dark apartment. There were towels, sweaters, and wool socks hanging to dry on the right. A large pot of what might actually had been potatoes on a wood burning stove on the left. She had never seen food cooked this way. The old women reached behind an old dirty dresser and pushed a button and the

dresser slid to the side revealing another door. She then opened the door and muttered something incoherent. Moon moved closer. The door led to another dark set of stairs going down even further. It could have been to a basement but there were way too many stairs for a normal basement. The women again just pointed and moon looked at her with a question on her face. After the woman gave no encouragement and just pointed again. She started down. After about the third step, the door closed hard behind her. Moon slowly descended.

She thought to herself, "This is where I am kidnapped and killed."

Outside down the block at the other end of the alley the two female detectives were following a beacon on their PDS's. It showed an icon of Moon's face and a map leading them to the alley. As soon as Moon went through the second door the signal disappeared. The detectives searched down the alley and then found themselves at the same set of stairs that led to the green door. They knocked but did not give the password. The same elderly lady answered the door.

"We are looking for Moon Cadel."

They showed the woman the picture. She spoke in Dagestani Russian.

The PDS translated, "What girl there is no girl. You can look around if you wish."

The apartment was so small and so full of junk that they only stepped in a little and looked around but then stepped back outside.

One of them spoke into their PDS, "Director Cadel."

Cadel answered, "Go ahead."

"We lost her."

At about half way down, Moon started hearing club music and screaming and yelling. After about thirty steps she was at the bottom and was met with another door. The music was louder now but still muffled by the door. She tried the knob and it opened. Suddenly she was blinded by light and loud music. She walked three steps and then rounded a corner. She was amazed at what she saw. It was some sort of exclusive club. It completely hung on the southern underside of the floating city. It was open with lots of glass, semi-visible metals, and open windows. The sun was setting off in the west and from this position on the southern end of the city was shining beautifully into the club. There was a mixture of strange music and even stranger occupants. In the city above, weapons were banned and tightly controlled but here were worn openly. She still had her backpack with her and she held it tight. She made her way through the club. There was a group of young elites dancing in the center. A number of VIP tables were lined along the outside. There was a band near the bar but also near the view. She approached the bar. No one seemed to even care that she was underage. There was blue and red lights that were moving and dancing with the music. As the sunset and the natural light from outside lowered the interior colored lights made it hard to see. The bar tender approached. He had a bare chest under a leather vest. He had some sort of jewelry that connected the piercings in his nipples one to another. He leaned forward and his skins color started to glow in the moonlight and she could clearly see his pointed ears near his buzz cut.

"What can I get you?"

Moon asked nervously, "I'll have a coco wine."

"You mean a Cacao Wine?"

"Yeah that."

The bar tender looked at a man at the end of the bar. The huge man named Truco was seven feet tall. He had on a long sleeve shirt with v neck collar and dress pants. He was bald and running along his head were hardened sections of bone that pierced out of his skin. They looked almost like natural armor appendages. And under the thin cloth of his shirt, the hardened bone tissue was also visible, especially where he had his sleeves rolled up. He approached Moon.

"The Theobroma drink is over five thousand years old."

She answered, "But I love chocolate."

"Come with me." Truco grunted.

She was almost as good of an intelligence officer as her father was in his younger days. This was before the Order of the Bliss had come to consume him. On the other end of the bar from Moon and Truco was the mysterious man that had saved Hanno and Moon from sure death in the Salty Tallywhacker. This time the suit he wore was the most unique deep blue color. As the darkness of night filled the club all of the Lua Elves lit up, including this man. Truco took Moon to a back office. When she passed through a narrow hall, it scanned her for weapons and electronics. It also synced with her PDS and had her identified. As the backpack passed the scanner, it brought up the short sword which alerted and was marked as a dangerous weapon. It also brought up a number of other items that were in the pack as hazardous. Many of which she herself was not aware of. An operator in a control room out of view reviewed the scan.

A voice came from the speaker, "Bag is not clear."

Truco put out his hand. His hand looked bigger than her whole head. Moon reluctantly handed it to him but then pulled it back slightly.

"I'll get this back right?"

She tried to sound confident and in charge.

He just said, "That's not up to me."

They entered in together. The office was luxuriant and full of bright colors including the most beautiful golden cloth that lined the walls. A thin man with a stripe lined suit sat with two women at each side. The women were dressed scantily and sitting lower than him on some sort of foam seats. He just stared at her. She started talking nervously.

"I am prepared to pay for a PDS removal and ground transportation to the beach."
Again he just looked at her. She saw all eyes were on her. Another man came from a back room and was now on her other side from Truco.

"I have credits, lots of them."

He interrupted her, "Oh you have credits, we like credits here don't we guys."
He had a thick accent she didn't recognize, it was not of the world she knew. He leaned forward and he had a number of facial tattoos and implants. Some looked natural but others were aesthetically added.

"I can have the credits...." She tried to take charge.

"No more talk young lady. I'll ask the questions."

Outside on the street the two detectives were determined to not give up. They had called in a number of security drones and security units to help with the search. A flying command post arrived and stationed over the block at the end of the alley thirty feet over the scene. It sent down a platform and the two detective's got in and went up. Inside the command post they began to see an area map start to form on virtual screens. The drones that were patrolling and circling the surrounding area started bring up security feeds and PDS tracers showing all of the individuals in the area and the path Moon had taken. The feeds show Moon go down the stairs at the end of the alley and through the door. There were three dimensional views of all of the surrounding buildings. But nothing other than a small apartment for the door she went through. Reviewing the video feeds of Moon's movements, they then saw a ghost appear in the alley.

"Look what's that?" One asked the operator.

"Not sure let me zoom in the surrounding cameras."

Again there was movement on the pixels on the screen but no one there. The shadow man was following behind Moon.

The other asked, "What about heat and DNA signature trails."

The operator adjusted and entered in several commands and then moved them up on the screen. All who had walked down that alley within the last day came up with vivid detail. It showed Moon, a cat behind a dumpster, a homeless man down around the corner, a delivery man on the adjoining street, and the two detectives. But still the nothing more for the ghost.

"Well maybe it's a signal error with the system I'll have to shut it down and do a systems check."

"You can do that later we need you on over watch."

Then the detective spoke into her PDS, "We need a tac team on Arrow and Downey Street."

We fast forward to the southern corner of

the city overlooking Arrow and Downey Street. There are great number of security personal who have completely shut down all of the surrounding streets. It would have seemed like an over response, unless you knew it was the director of the Bliss's daughter who had runaway. Who knows what the enemies of Bliss could do with her.

Inside the exclusive bar owners office.

"How exactly are you going to get me all these credits you speak about?"

Moon motions to her backpack, "I've got twenty thousand in gold certified city credits already printed in a small leather pouch."

Truco dug the pouch out, opened it and thumbed through the discs shaped credits. Then he threw the pouch on the boss's desk.

"I tell you what I'm going to do. I'm going to pay this to myself... as a finder's fee for finding a brand new girl to work in my stables."

The group around the boss laughed a creepy sickening laugh. Moon was right, she was being kidnapped and about to disappear into the underground network of prostitution slave trade.

The edge of the city was so massive it resembled the side of a mountain but was made out of unique synthetic metals and plastics running along the whole hundred foot thick structure. A long this edge were numerous mechanical devices including intakes connecting and facilitating the cities utilities and maintenance. A very heavy fog rolled up to and over the side of the cities southern edge. Up onto the street. Several of the intake vents appeared to be blocked. The clouds passed right over the edge like a wave. Up on the street the fog drifted and filled up the streets and lower buildings. The two detectives were down at the entrance of the alley near the command post. On the other end of the alley was the stairway and door that Moon went through. They were standing by as a tactical team unloaded and zip lined down on streams of lights from their tactical vehicle. Each one dressed in armor TAC gear with laser and shock weapons landed and formed two lines along the entrance of the alley. The fog filled up the area around them first at their feet but then up and over their vehicle that was stationed fifty feet above the ground.

"Ops I need thermals up and sent to all response units."
The operator switched several switches and the detectives and the operators had the system send first to their wrist but then up to their eyes where they had thermal scans of the alley that penetrated the fog.

"Move out." One of the detectives spoke out over her coms.
On the edge of the city four subs, similar to the one seen outside of the Salty Tallywhacker but longer, hovered along the edge of the city. Side doors opened and dark figures moved out into the fog. As the city security force moved tactically down the

alley, the command post operator saw a set of dark images in the fog that were not showing up on thermals.

"Tac one you have bogies coming up from behind you."

Up in the command post the operator was surprised by the door opening behind him. He assumed it was one of the detectives coming to complain.

"You know I didn't make the fog. But I did found out that intake twenty seven and twenty four are malfunctioning. I've already contacted city services..."

From the opening of the room a huge dark black beast lowered its head as it entered the control room. Its body was black and full of sinewy muscles. It floated rather than walked slowly behind him. He sensed something was in the room and reached for a panic button. But before his hand could come down on the button, a long black tentacle wrapped around his wrist and pulled so hard his whole body turned and flew towards the beast. Now he was hanging several meters off the ground. We track up from his feet and alongside his body was a huge vampire looking beast with numerous tentacles that were now all moving and grabbing at his body as he struggled to get free. The man was seized and wrapped up in such a way that no limb was free to move. He started to scream and a last dark tentacle came from behind him and wrapped up his mouth. And now from this close view the underside of the tentacles suction cups can be seen moving and sucking at him as the tentacle strengthens its grasp. Pulling the man forward now the hood of the beast could be seen. The huge head opened with a vertical seem down. Inside the darkness was a deep smoke and a red eye. The man's face was full of terror as he was pulled into the darkness of the hood of the beast.

The TAC team was almost at the end of the street when the command post lost stability and crashed down at the entrance of the alley.

'Kaaaboooom!'

A blast wave knocked down the officers and sent fire exploding up the sides of buildings and out into the alley. From inside the bar the explosion was not pronounced and many didn't even feel it. But the mysterious man did. He got up casually and made his way toward the hall to the back office. Out on the street the TAC team and the two detectives had just shook of the shock and were starting to stand and orient themselves when a wave of the green sea lizard looking creatures attacked them from out of the fog from all sides. The dark beast moved with them and also grabbed and threw security officers with his huge tentacles as he moved down the alley. His figure had changed to that of a tall dark man. But his movement was still that of a beast.

Truco inside the office felt something too and looked at the boss. And with an unspoken look

Truco left the office to the outer corridor. The mysterious man had just arrived and was now standing toe to toe with Truco.

"What do you think you are doing?" Truco said with a thick accent.

The man then said in an ancient language something. And held his hand at about the height of Moon. The man just looked at him.

Then the man translated, "No you don't understand, what I said was I'm looking for a friend she's about this tall."

He again put his hand at about Moon's height. Truco turned his gaze to the man's right hand. That was the only distraction he needed. Our mysterious friend drew from under his tails the first short sword with his other hand and sliced the man at his ribs. His knife cut flesh and landed hard on Truco's hardened armor bones underneath. Truco didn't even flinch and slightly smiled. Truco's shirt was ripped and he tore off the rest revealing huge amounts of exposed armored up bone and muscle all over his body. Then the mysterious man lowered his head but locked his eyes on Truco. He drew from within a strange blue energy. It was the same energy that Hanno had used to impart his abilities to Moon. This energy moved like water but was like blue wisps of living light. The energy formed patterns and designs as it filled his hands and body. The energy empowered his body and his whole body began to shine a deep blue color. He then spun and pulled his other short sword. He was moving and spinning like a dancer might move and sliced with the sword in his right hand. The large man put his forearm out and this time when the sword came down on bone it actually sparked like metal hitting metal. Truco size filled up the corridor as he exploded forward like a linebacker at the man. The mysterious man moved his arms and body quickly and as he moved the blue energy trailed and moved with him. He moved in such a way that the suit coat and tails moved and spun off his arms and body. Then the coat wrapped up the man's head and he moved low and quick behind the man. Both swords then came up in violence and stabbed with lethal accuracy the man's lower back where no visible bones were at. Truco arched in deep pain and then dropped dead. The control room operator was reading a holographic book and only noticed the fight after it was in full swing. He reached out his hand to a panic alarm and the mysterious man pulled both swords and thrust his right one through the wall and pinned the man's hand to the wall. He waved his other sword at him.

"aaah open the door please."
The man unlocked the door. He pulled the sword and moved through the door right as several green sea beasts and their dark lord entered the back of the bar.

CHAPTER 8: 3X+1

Hanno was standing on top of a metallic sombrero that capped the head of the three story tall Pedro statue. The bright yellow had faded and was now a dull gray. Attached to and built behind it was the tower that stretched up to the bottom of the city. Although the path was sealed and blocked. Looking up at the bottom of New Atlanta all he could think of was Moon. The bottom did create a darkness on the land below. But it also provided a unique view. Looking up on the city was like looking up on a great spaceship. There were sparks and energy surges. A soft glow of the new energy source that emanated from the vortex sights. Constant steam exhausts from giant pressure valves and gears and shafts spinning from the mechanics. All the science and technology it took to keep the city afloat and functioning properly. Hanno saw as Granger climbed the metal ladder that went up the center of metal structure. The tower not only looked up to New Atlanta's underbelly but it also looked down on the Oasis. As Granger came along Hanno's side he at first looked up where Hanno was looking but then looked down over his domain.

"You know what makes Grounder's different?" Granger said with pride.

Hanno shook his head and now changed his view to the complex below.

"The word 'human' comes from 'humus' which means 'from the earth' or 'from the ground.' Our common ground as human beings is that we are all 'from the ground.' Many up there have forgotten that."

"I wouldn't know. I've never been." Hanno looked up.

Granger continued, "Humans are dust, holy dust of God, and to dust we will one day return. We need to embrace our dustiness, our mortality, our dying, is an important part of the spiritual life."

It had been weeks since Hanno first arrived at the Oasis. Granger had been stalling. Hanno was granted a temporary visa which came in the form of a laser tattoo on his wrist that glowed in the dark. It was in the shape of the Oasis center. He rubbed it while he listed to Granger and looked out over Oasis.

"Do you know what the Bliss death ceremony consist of?"

Hanno didn't.

"They aerosol their bodies with Taoide particles. Then they release them and the bodies float up and out of the atmosphere. Imagine how many arrogant SOB's are floating in the sky."

DANIEL J. NESHER

"What is it about the Bliss that you hate so much?" Hanno asked honestly.

"Hanno when Bliss came along everything changed. My Great, great, grandad was one of the first survivors that had found Oasis. He and several of his kin had hiked from a settlement in West Virginia. It was brutal and hard in the outlands. Nothing lives there. They scraped by off of desert rats and sand crickets. Then He came to the Oasis. New Atlanta was new. It had only launched the year before. Word had been sent out to all of the wasteland. Settlers like him came from all over."

Below them a night watch was switching out on one of the wall mounted gun posts. Hanno was finding himself drawn in to Grangers story.

"I don't remember my past. But I know I am not from here."

Granger had spent many days talking to Hanno. Hanno was given a job in the crops below ground. He didn't mind it. The moisture levels were high due to the overhead sprinkler system. If he had to be so far from the ocean being under active sprinklers on a regular basis helped. But he longed to see Moon. He needed to leave.

"Right you washed up on the shore. Maybe you fled to the sea from somewhere down south like the Caribbean."

"I don't know but everything and everyone here feels different to me."

Granger leaned in, "Well what do you think

about God?"

"I believe in an all-powerful Creator. How can you look at the ocean and not."

Granger smirked, "I've never been."

"What do you believe about Jesus?"

Hanno rubbed his chin, "Seth my friend used to tell me about Earth's ancient Christian religion."

Granger brought out from a satchel he had on his shoulder.

"Here."

He handed him a small black bible.

"Thousands of years ago America was ruled by capitalism."

Hanno looked at him strangely.

"You know free trade, free markets?"

Hanno had no idea.

"Well anyways it was the closest thing to free will ever. Each man or woman let their desires speak with each dollar they spent. But it did have a nasty little side effect in rewarding the most ruthless and driven. The left side of the coin complained about fairness. At the time there was also lots of division over social issues. So as it is among humans, war broke out and we nearly destroyed ourselves. As we began to rebuild, the Order of Bliss came along. It was a powerful force of those who believed only in Social Justice and Equableness of finances. And it also was made up of the intellectual elite. Ideas of free markets were gone. Freedom of religion, gone. It actually became illegal to believe in God. Those who claimed to fight for the poor and social outcasts took power. As always, power corrupts. Suddenly over night the water that flowed down the pipe was turned off. And we grounders not only were not being offered passage to the city. We were left for dead."

Hanno looked at the huge tower that connected Oasis to the city above.

"But we have water."

"Yeah only because we highjack it out of their system."

"That's why my mission for you is so important. Come on I want to show you something."

The bar that hung beneath New Atlanta was under attack and the mysterious man was being held at gunpoint by the bar owner in the back room. He had some sort of rifle pointing at him. Moon was bound and shoved in the corner behind the desk. One of the girls was holding a knife on Moon. But the manner she was holding it, told him she did not know what she was doing. Moon and the man caught eyes. He showed her kind eyes. He replaced the swords in the sheaths attached to his back. Underneath the sheaths aligned with his belt at his lower back was a very large gun that looked like the cross between an old 18th century flintlock and a laser weapon. It had lots of electronics and metal seams that looked new and energized. Now with his coat off he was wearing black pants, black boots and a black dress shirt with a stylish collar.

"What you need to ask yourself is one thing." The mysterious man lowered his hands to his waist.

The bar owner had crazy untrusting eyes, "What is that?"

"Do you have time to fight me and also the horde of Dacacian warriors that have just entered your establishment?"

Dacacians, like Lua Elves, were thought to be a myth. Ever since the fall of earth with the great wars it was rumored that new creatures and new technology had somehow arrived to the earth. But now were thought to be only legend. In fact The Order of the Bliss first aligned and allied with the Dacacians. But this alliance quickly fell apart. There exists no writings whether in electronic or paper from of this history. Legend tells that the Bliss took the technology and then used it against the Dacacians. They attempted to purge all non-humans from the planet. And when they ran out of green and blue adversaries they moved on to the human kind that did not agree with their ways.

That got the bar owners attention. Distracted he brought up a holographic screen and he could see his employees and patrons were proned out on the floor and the bar was full of green warriors. Suddenly the mysterious man pulled the pistol from behind his lower back and it exploded and blew the man's head against the back wall. Then with his other hand pulled his sword and stabbed the man to his left before he knew what had just happened. He then lastly pointed the gun at the woman and she quickly dropped the knife and put her hands up moving toward the other corner with the other girl.

He holstered both the knife and the gun, "My name is Demetris Androsis. I am a Tarchanjan Noble here to help you and Hanno."

Just hearing Hanno's name gave her instant relief. Behind them they could hear some of the attackers making their way down the corridor.

Moon stood, "Thank you."

Demetris was a man in his forties with thick well-groomed brown hair and a distinctive looking face. He first fortified the door by tipping over a cabinet. The office had no windows but he then saw a seam under the desk. They moved the desk together and he was able to pull up a panel.

"An escape hatch. Boy do I love these Kazenska's."

He pulled up the hatch and Moon almost forgot her backpack. She grabbed it and then went in first and he went behind her. He closed the hatch right as the Dacacians entered the office. The hatch led to a small corridor. They had to move on their hands and knees. On every turn they went at a downward angle. Then the escape tunnel opened up on a utilities corridor under the city. Now they could finally stand. The Dacacians had found the hatch and where coming out of the small corridor behind them and opened fire. Their rifles and handguns shot out bolts of lightning cracking and exploding all around them. Moon screamed and Demetris moved her around a corner and drew and fired from his gun. His long handgun shot a projectile that was energized and exploded and shot through one creature and then also through the one behind him killing both. Now Demetris and Moon were in a full sprint. They ran down a long corridor and then another. With each turn more and more of the Dacacians creatures poured out behind them. Demetris energized himself again and the energy seemed to move and swivel around both Moon and him causing them to run faster. At the end of the corridor they hit a dead end and literally slammed against a small wall. The impact caused a piece of metal to pop off. Now they were standing at an opening looking down thousands of feet. It was the far bottom edge of the city and nothing but sky in front of them and earth below.

Demetris turned to Moon, "Get behind me."

He moved his hands in a pattern that was clearly some sort of ritual but also looked like a master of some ancient art. The blue energy moved out of his body and then moved with his hands and started forming a blue shield across the corridor. The beasts were stacking up and firing on them, but none of the bolts could penetrate his shield.

"If we were in water my shield would be

stronger but here we are running out of time."
Moon could not imagine what he was saying.
The Dacacian weapons were dark and mysterious.
They had wisps of metal that spiked forward and
along the barrel. The handle and grip were set
in the center. The barrel was bisected and went
forward toward the target. But also behind the
grip was another set of barrels. Demetris then
turned and moved his hands again but this time
small movements of his left finger over his right
forearm. It formed a small set of designs and
symbols. At the other end of the hall the dark
black beast full of tentacles arrived and moved in
front of his warriors.

Moon saw him and shrieked, "Look out!"
As the great black beast moved down the narrow
hall its tentacles moved and searched the wall
almost as if they moved with their own will.
The hooded head started to open and the single
large red eye was fixed on them. As the beast
arrived at the blue energy shield its tentacles filled
the shield, fighting, pushing, and searching for a
way through. The beast's one eye was locked on
Moon and she went into a trance. Demetris kept
looking out the opening and could fill the beast
and the shield failing. Right as the shield phased
out, Demetris with one quick move drew from his
back the huge powerful gun and shot straight at
the beasts head and grabbed Moon with the other
arm and pulled them both out the opening. The
black beast dodge the shot and lunged at them and

forced its head and four of its tentacles out to try and grab them while the rest of his tentacles held on to the sides of the opening. They fell away and Moon came out of the trance and suddenly realized she was falling. But before she even had time to scream Demetris wrist lit up with blue energy that was tracking an image of his ship. As the ship got closer, a small icon on his arm showed its arriving below them. A roof door opened and now a light tractor beam surrounded them and pulled them in. The ship was long, sleek, and silver with no windows. There were only a line of seams going up the front and over the top. Each seam was energized with the same mysterious blue energy. At the back the ship was full of power from two large energy jets, one on top and one lower. Both jets had additional smaller vents below and behind each. The ship was so sleek and smooth that as it exploded forward, it disappeared into the sky.

Granger and Hanno were underground. They made their way through the fields of corn and then enter the Mathematician's Lab. Jerry was finishing adjustments to a device. It looked like a circular table with purple and black plates that ran vertically interconnected with silver coils going horizontally. He then pushed a button and nothing happened.

Jerry then speaking to himself as Granger and Hanno walked in, "Himmeldonnerwetter!" He then banged a wrench on the side and the device came to life. He quickly stood and watched as the device shot up a three dimensional image of the whole solar system mixed with engineering schematics. There was also formulas and foreign symbols moving and surrounding the images. They were all moving and living as they mixed in beams of an array of purples, blues, and red colors. Jerry stood rubbing his hands together watching it unfold.

"Jerry tell Hanno about 3X+1."

Jerry adjusted some virtual switches in the air with his hands and the projections above the machine changed to more math formulas with graphs.

Jerry then spoke never taking his eyes off the projections, "3X+1 was an impossible math problem that the Luas taught Jerry how to solve." Jerry often spoke about himself in the third person.

"Also known as the Collatz Conjecture. It was considered the most dangerous math problem in the world. A simple conjuncture that no one could solve. Breaking the 421 loop was impossible. Jerry spent many days working to find the end. Then Jerry was told about the closed loop cloud stack exchange that led to the strange attractor." Jerry spoke low but kept calculating and adjusting the formula. The math graphs and formulas then changed to molecules on the devise. And from the images of the molecules energy exploded. The same energy that held up the city and floated the buildings. Hanno saw but didn't understand.

Granger explained, "It changed everything. We found it everywhere. Not unlike the Fibonacci sequence, the Collatz Conjecture was the key to our new energy source. Everything we understood about atoms, protons, and electrons were so oversimplified. For example we learned that a proton is not just a shape of let's say like a billiard ball, but it's actually a cloud of electrically charged quartz held together by gluons."

Jerry got excited as he watched the projection and raised his voice, "The harmonics of the Zeta function changed the directional wave and frequency. It opened Jerry's mind to multiple complex dimensional math."

Granger then to Jerry, "Jerry calm down. Eyes Jerry."

Then like a little kid Jerry turned to Granger and visibly calmed down.

Granger while maintaining eye contact with Jerry continued to talk to Hanno, "The Luas chose Jerry because of his gifts."

Jerry repeated after him now in a lower calmer tone, "Jerry has gifts."

"They chose him and it was this same beautiful small man whose engineering and math skills got New Atlanta off the ground."

Hanno got it, "You mean he is the inventor of Taoide Energy?"

"Yep if it weren't for the Jerry and the Luas we would still all be in the wastelands. And after the city was afloat. And the Order of the Bliss took over. He was deemed as not worthy."

Hanno, "That's horrible. What does all this have to do with me?"

Granger then motioned something to Jerry and he began making new adjustments to the device. Up on the devise an image of the water tower formed. But not just a three dimensional image but it showed the active and moving parts on the inside of the tower. Inside the tower was rapidly moving and surging water currents. Then the virtual screens image showed math formulas, velocities, geometries, and calculations. Then a very small image of Hanno appeared. It was an image of Hanno with all of his tentacles out. He was moving and swimming his way up the tower.

CHAPTER 9: REFUGEE CITY

Deep underwater the sleek stream-lined ship of Demetris Androsis moved smoothly through a deep sea trench. On both sides of the ship were caverns of underwater mountains. The ships energy of blue and white glowed and was emanating from the sleek lines that ran bow to aft like glowing tiger stripes built into the aluminous white metal beast. The inside of the ship was a lot larger than you would think from the outside. The helm of the ship was in the middle of the ship. Four swiveling captain's chairs sat at the four corners of a circular bridge full of controls. Completely surrounding the helm was a three hundred and sixty degree field of vision. It wasn't screens that provided the view. But more like vivid windows all along the ships walls looking out into the sea in all directions. From the outside there were no visible windows. The view was made from some sort of projections and it made the walls from the inside appear see through. Demetris was sitting in the forward driver's seat side and was busy at navigating the ship. Moon was sitting in the aft passenger side seat. She was slowly spinning around in the chair. She was looking out at all of the sights. From outside in the sea the view was dark, deep, and slightly green. But from inside the ship the view was similar to Hanno's sight, clear, bright, and beautiful; full of numerous sights of flora and fauna. It reminded her of Hanno.

"Tell me again where Hanno is?"
Demetris was looking for something and running a search on one of his devises.

Distracted, "Under the city."

"What does that mean?"

"Under New Atlanta, you know in the wastelands."

"I've never been outside the city. Is it dangerous?"

"Oh yes very."
The look on her face went from playful to dreadful in two seconds flat. He remembered that human's emotions were so fragile and tried to encourage her.

"But he is destined for adventure and my sources have told me that he is adapting well."

"Why can't we go get him now again?"

"We first need to talk to Deyva."
As a teenager can be, she had stacks and stacks of questions he was not prepared to answer.

"Hey can you help me. Go to the aft and start up Nerwin."

Moon happily got up and made her way to the back. Right behind the helm was four private sleeping pods with queen size beds and entertainment slash work stations. Then she passed the galley with a poker table and chairs, a larger refrigerator, food storage shelves, and of course coffee pot all built in and secure. Over the poker table was engraved in very old metal 'Cheonia'. Under it was a picture of four Luas and a child in traditional royal dress.

"What does Cheonia stand for?"

"It's pronounced 'Kelonia. It was taken from my father's ship. It was a Royal War ship that was destroyed. I named my ship after it."

At the back of the ship was a mechanical room. But to call it mechanical was a misnomer. It really was something else. There were tubes of light and energy that she had never seen before. luminescent sections for operational controls like the Sectosonar, a type of sonar that not only captures and uses sound but light and wave energy as well. Then there was the dive chamber below her. She saw lots of dials, controls, and devices but nothing labeled "Nerwin."

"I don't see it. Where is it?"

He spun his chair around and although it was a long ship they could still see each other through the other rooms.

"Right there near your left hand."

She moved her hand along the wall while watching him. She still had no idea was he was talking about.

Along the back passenger side of the ships walls were pipes, lines, and then a circular section with more pipes, tubes, and lines. As she moved hand she came to a built-in hand size switch.

"There that's Nerwin.   Hit that power button and then pull the release lever."
She still didn't see it. But she did see something that sort of looked like a button near a lever.

"Oh well I hope I don't blow up the ship."
She hit the button and then started to pull on the lever. The lever was heavy and she had to grab it with both hands to pull it down. A burst of pressure scared her and she jumped back.

"Oh my!"
Demetris was back working on his project. Then steam and air could be seen to be coming from the edges of a large circular object embedded below the lever attached to the wall. Then movement. Then suddenly the huge metal ball jumped out of the wall and landed on two feet.

"DSV Nerwin reporting for duty."

Moon looked over her shoulder toward Demetris but then quickly back to Nerwin.

"What is it?"
Arms then came from somewhere along its circular center. Nerwin was a metallic ball in the shape of a small deep ocean vessel but he had two legs and feet coming out the bottom of the vessel and two arms and hands out the lower front.   There was a large "O" ring on top which

looked like it once was used to hoist him by a crane into a ship. There were steel cable ropes tied and strapped around his body. Pipes and tubes sticking out as sensors. Two lights attached to what might be considered his chin. And for a face was what looked like a port door that was replaced with a heavy duty screen. His face booted up and then the most curious face of an old skipper captain showed up on his screen.

"I am a DSV or Deep Ship Vessel. Nuclear class NRI. During the war I was used as deep ocean counter surveillance and stealth operations. I was a spy."

Up to that point he sounded like a strange blend of old skipper and electronic computer voice but when he said 'I was a spy.' He sounded like a little kid.

Moon liked him instantly, "Oh you were a spy. Weren't you special?"

Nerwin waddled toward her and reach out his hand to shake. All of his body was a mix of heavy deep sea metals and some new materials. Demetris had obviously made many changes and upgrades.

Demetris then ordered, "Nerwin launch and find Port 213."

"Copy that Captain."

Then to Moon, "You better head back to the helm."

Moon slowly backed away and as soon as she passed the portal entrance to the Mechanical

117

section an invisible force field sealed off the room and then another force field covered the dive chamber floor door. The door then opened and Nerwin launched into the sea.

Moon found her way back up to the helm. Demetris had on the front view an image looking down below the ship at a huge sea rock wall. The two cavern walls on the left and right met right in front of them. Demetris flipped up on a side panel the chart overlay of the area. On the chart behind the wall was what looked like a very complex city. Nerwin approached the wall where it met the sea floor. There was nothing special about this section of sea wall. Where Nerwin was standing even with the higher resolution view it looked like a bunch of rocks over grown with sea creatures. Nerwin brushed off a section and then appeared to be entering or pushing something on a panel. Then the panel first came to life with a bright green energy. This energy grew out from the panel up high and created a large oval seam. Then the energy filled the doors and a pattern of characters and symbols glowed with the green energy. The door opened. The ship moved forward towards the entrance door. As it passed over Nerwin, a beam grabbed him and pulled him back into the ship. Passing through the door a closer view showed the doors design and it was clearly manufactured and not a natural formation. From the sea above, the area looked like long, deep cracks and crevasses cut deep into the seafloor. But from their view within the ship, the deep cracks revealed tall sides of large buildings built into the sea walls. With vertical columns full of windows and porches. The large decorative columns lined each section of units. Pass the entrance the tall deep sea streets went off in every direction. They were moving straight down Center Street. The ship was moving at the mid level of the buildings with forty floors above and forty floors below. Moon leaned up out of her seat and sat on her feet to get a better view. As they passed, Moon saw creatures living and occupying the apartments in the walls. She saw a child playing with a small sea creature. The child threw a cylinder toy and it cut through the sea with ease. It came very close to the outside of the ship and thus right in front of her view. And a creature, somewhere between an otter and a fish, swam up to it and grabbed it with little hands. It froze in place for only a moment. Then just as fast swam back to the boy fetching the toy. Moon was now up on her knees with her hand against the wall/screen.

"ahhh, did you see that? He was so cute."
Demetrius was on alert and did not in fact see it. Below at the seafloor of the city was crafted walkways and sea gardens. People were talking and walking and living in the outside spaces.

"Who are they?" She asked inquisitively.
"Luas."
"Elves?"
"Yes, abandoned and betrayed years ago.

We'll not all Luas. Some Grogalls, some Hvalurs, and some humans, but mostly Luas."

And even as he said it she could see the different species. By this time Nerwin made his way up to the helm. He walked by a table and due to his size knocked off Demetris coffee.

'Crash'

"I'm sorry Captain."

"Darn it Nerwin you know what I said about not coming forward of the galley."

"But I wanted to see the girl."

Moon was already helping clean up the mess, "I'm Moon."

"How pretty, Moon, I like it."

"Well I like you Nerwin."

Then Nerwin's screen face blushed and then smiled.

"Quiet we are entering the southern district."

Moon made her way back to her seat. Nerwin was standing looking over her shoulder.

"Southern District of what?"

"We are in Anchali Amara refugee city. It means hand of God. It's several thousand years old."

"How does no one know about it?"

"Well it helps that the seas are no longer navigable, at least on the surface. If the powers that control your world knew, they would seek to destroy us because we are deemed 'outside the Order'."

"Why?"

"Well most likely because the Luas have a rich history of faith. And any form of religion was outlawed by the Bliss. The Bliss started as an order of diversity, tolerance, and community but has somehow become a controlling order of intolerance."

Moon felt something on her side. Nerwin had slid a hot cup of coco on the table near her.

"Oh Nerwin thank you."

"You're welcome Moon."

He then gave Demetris another cup of coffee to replace the one he spilled.

"I was never taught religion or faith?" she stated honestly.

"But I did have a friend who was a... Christian? And we would talk sometimes when no one else was around."

"See that is sad. You have lived seventeen years on this earth and you don't even know your creator."

Moon scratched her head, "But I thought the earth evolved."

"The Luas believe that the creator, created all worlds. As soon as the Luas heard about the Christian faith. We studied your bible and found the God of the Jews and the father of Jesus sounded an awful lot like the God of our world."

"And Hanno believes this?"

"He did when he was younger."

He paused and looked out into the city.

Then said to her, "When a Lua meets another Lua we say 'Hola Ke Akua."

Moon repeated it, "Hola Ke Akua."

Then Nerwin repeated it, "Hola Ke Akua." They laughed a little.

"It means, 'Water of God' or 'God's love." They started to descend. The row of buildings they just entered then opened up into a large open full circle. The buildings still had residential areas above but at ground level were shops, stores, and communal areas. There was also lots of open space. The open circular area was easy the size of a small city itself. There were numerous oceanic vessels parked everywhere some sealed and airtight and others open or seawater full. They parked along the far north side of the circle and floated about twenty feet off the seafloor.

"Nerwin you have the helm."

"Yes sir Captain."

Nerwin returned to his parking hub at the back of the ship and his screen changed from the skipper face to a ship operations AI.

"There's a changing room in your pod."

And with that, Demetris went into his pod.

The pods were stacked vertically alongside one another. Two on one side and two on the other. When she entered into the pod on one end was a queen size bed. She opened a storage door and found clothing. She held it in her hand and we just see her face with this 'O no this is going to be interesting' look. They both came out of the pods at the same time. The outfits were not quite scuba suits but tight and form fitting. They were brownish green and were thick and insulated. They also were full of armor embedded into the material. On Demetris suit he had additional layers on his upper body. Along the front and back were covered in armor. The whole design of the material appeared as the bones and muscles of some great beast. He had pads and pockets; some were functional and others decorative and traditional. Attached to the back armor were his two short swords. He also had his very powerful handgun across his lower back below the swords. The armor on his upper body looked like it was a blend of shark skin and thick leather. He had a chest piece that was sleeveless. On his forearms and upper biceps were bracers made from the same material. The layer of armor around his neck and down his spine appeared to be powered and energized. But at his midsection just a swimming shorts. Moon speculated if they allowed for tentacles like Hanno had. She was right. Demetris pulled from his back the pistol checked the mechanism and prepared it.

"Where's mine?" She joked. Then "Will it work underwater?"

He smiled, "It was made for water. It's a miracle it works in the air."

They were standing over the dive chamber. He moved his hands in a similar motion as he did when he first summoned the ship. And his blue particle energy moved out from his body and over Moon as Hanno had done before.

"Oh boy I'm a mermaid again."

He looked at her and was very serious, "Moon this is for your protection. Without the Plava Boya you would be instantly crushed by the pressure at this level. If something happens to me you have minutes to get somewhere safe."

"What's going to happen to you?"

"We are going somewhere that is, well, not safe." He said awkwardly.

He then approached and checked her suit.

"This is for breathing if the Plava fails."

He pointed to a device near her neck.

"Just push this button and it will do all the work. The suit will protect you for approximately two minutes and then you are on your own."

With that he opened the chamber and they floated down below the ship into the sea. They touched down on the surface. It felt hard on Moon's feet and looked like marble. The Plava Boya or blue energy also changed something about their buoyancy. It was the way the energy interact with the pressure at this level. They were walking on the floor like on a city street. They turned toward the center and at the center of the commercial southern district was a circular building that looked more like a fort. It was about half as tall as the surrounding buildings. It was made of something that looked like ancient stone, but had architecture design too. As they got closer it appeared more like an octagon than a circle. On each corner was a tower from base to top. The towers made each side look like the entrance to a great fort. On the street Moon loved the view under the Plava Boya. It was so clear and so beautiful. She looked all around at the buildings and the different species. She breathed in and out. She saw water move but felt air although it was water. Moon then looked up and way above them was the sea far above. She could see the top of the buildings and the opening the circle made.

"Why couldn't we just have flown the ship in from above?"

It was a good question but he was slightly distracted and had his head and eyes on a pivot.

"The deep sea currents would crush the ship and everything inside."

He kept walking and she just murmured under her breath, "Oh crush you, I see."

From above the powerful currents rushed and moved violently across the top of the cracks of the city. Due to the designs of the tops of the city and the Sea Mountains none of these powerful currents could breach into the city. The design created a sort of protected roof to the whole region. They walked through the two double doors on the southern side. Inside the fort like building looked larger than the outside. Inside was a huge industrial factory updated and modified into a dance club. The outer sections all around were restaurants, bars, and other entertainment areas. In the center was an open area with ceilings that went all the way up. In this open area in the very middle was a pyramid with a huge engraved eye at the top of all three sides. And at the very top of the pyramid was a DJ playing music. But strangely the music really vibrated through the water and you could feel it in your whole body. Past the entrance on Moon's right she saw an 'Air bar'. A self enclosed area with no water but air. There were humans and non-humans in it. The humans had their deep sea suits hanging in the corner of an entrance chamber. A robotic squid with multiple arms was serving them drinks. They passed it and went to the far left side. They stood on a plate that then lifted them up to the forth level. Moon watched as partiers danced on the dancefloor below but also danced and floated in the sea around the pyramid. One very beautiful Lua woman moved in a loose dress. She had all of her tentacles out. And as her body and dress moved, it seemed almost in slow motion and Moon looked on how beautiful it seemed. Up on the forth level they sat at a table. When a server came Demetris leaned in and told her something in private. Their table was on the edge of the balcony and Moon was fascinated with all the sights and sounds. The great number of creatures were amazing too. Mostly Luas moving, swimming, and glowing blue in the sea. But also a great many other creatures. There were several men and women who looked like Truco, the large man Demetris fought in New Atlanta. But they had less clothing. Now with just small tight shirts, small shorts and no shoes their true shape and forms were visible. They were a large race with visibly hardened bones throughout their whole bodies. They had webbed enlarged feet and fin like tails. The bones were shaped backward and were hydrodynamic in the water.

"Who are we looking for again?" Moon asked while still looking out on all the activity.

"Deyva."

"Who is Deyva?"

"She is a priestess of Atlas."

"What's an Atlas?"

"Atlas is the first Lua that Akua, ah God made."

"Like Adam in the bible?"

"Yes like Adam. I thought the Order didn't allow religious studies."

"They don't the same friend who used to talk with me about faith gave me a bible. So I kept it and have been reading it secretly."

"You would be arrested if you were ever caught. And most likely sent to the Ground."

"I guess I'm a rebel for God."

Demetris like that saying. Right then a huge man came up and sat down at their table. He looked to be half man but also half manatee. He had thick layers of fat and big whiskers but a man's face. Instead of a large dorsal fin he had two legs with fin like feet. He more like swam over rather than walk until he got to the table and he sat down.

"I hear you are looking for Deyva."

Demetris turned to Moon, "Hey can you get us three sunrise-down drinks?"

Moon got up and saw them talking intently. She approached a bar tender that was a Dacacian but not a warrior a civilian. He was green and did have reptilian scales and lizard like form. But no armored uniform and no muscles. He was actually quite skinny and had a goofy looking face. He even appeared juvenile. Moon looked at him funny.

"What's so funny?"

"Aren't you a little young to be a bartender?"

"If two hundred and twenty two years old is young."

She shook her head realizing age of other species was a mystery to her.

"Oh yeah I guess. I need three sunrise-down drinks."

The bartender instantly went to work and within minutes handed her three drinks. They were in tall fat glasses with a rubber looking top. The drink was bright red and orange but that wasn't the strange thing about the drinks. She looked closer and there was something swimming inside with four sets of eyes.

"Eh gross."

She came back to the table and handed out the drinks.

CHAPTER 10: BARON VON BLAVALOTSKI

Hanno was sitting on the edge of a circular manmade pool. It was much larger than a pool and more like an above ground well with low sides. Jerry the Mathematician was standing near the well. Hanno was sitting on the edge with his feet in the water. As he swished his feet back and forth his feet transformed into tentacles and then back to feet with each swish. A little bit of blue energy came off of him and lit up the water. When Jerry saw it, he moved his hands in excitement. Down a long row of corn crops Granger approached them. The well was at the far end of the agricultural section of the Oasis.

"Are you ready Hanno?" Granger asked.

"Yeah I think so."

"Remember to empty the middle chamber you must first prime the pressure pump and then release the middle lever."

"Yep we've been over it a number of times.

And once I do this, I can use the center tube to get back to the city?"

"Yes. It will open for all of us, ... all sorts of possibilities."

Hanno jumped in the water and was wading effortlessly.

"Forty meters down and one thousand two hundred and ninety seven meters up." Jerry said under his breath."

As he said it he pictured it, it became visible in front of him with his mathematical imagination. Hanno swam down and his body transformed. His upper body still a man but different full of muscles and strength. His lower body full of long beautiful blue striped tentacles. He looked majestic. He power swam down and then started his journey up the main tower that connected Oasis to New Atlanta. Within the large tower was a center tube. It too went up the whole length from top to bottom. In this tube, they used the same energy that held up the city to lift up survivors. But now it was a dark, rusted space. Up, up, up Hanno went with ease. Swimming back and forth and circling the central metal tube that ran up the middle playfully like a dolphin. While swimming, the blue energy filled his body and even lit up the markings on his chest. The Boya then traveled throughout his body into what looked like natural blue tattoos on his arms and torso. He reached the top in no time. He found the mechanisms and started the process Granger and Jerry had showed him. He leveraged his tentacles against the side of the wall and pulled with his might. A huge pressure sound released and water could be heard to be rushing out of the middle tube. While the water near Hanno remained. He began his descent back down the well. Granger, Jerry and several of his security had moved above ground near a port door outside the tower. Jerry listened and calculated the volumes of water flushing out of the system. And when the sound of rushing water stopped. Jerry knew it a moment before it was complete. They opened a large side door at the tower behind Pedro. There was a lateral tube that passed through the outer part that was full of water and led to the inner tube. Here Granger then opened another port door. Granger stuck his head in the opening. It was in deed empty thanks to Hanno. Along the side of the tube wall was a metal ladder that was used if the energy lift went down or was not working. The metal latter went all the way up and the path into the city was clear.

Pulling up to a parking hub at the center club at the Southern District of Anchali Amara were three medium size dark subs and one large sub. Again due to the massive size of this center once they landed, they all appeared small. But they were still the largest vessels parked in the area. A concierge approached the large sub. The side door opened and out walked an entourage of Dacacian and Malrac warriors. The concierge stood still. Then came out the dark beast. It was in the form of a dark man with a heavy cloak and dark hood. But still appeared to glide rather than walk as it made its way down the platform.

"Baron Blavalotski, so nice to see you again. Your normal villa?"

"Oh you are too kind, just call me Blav. No not this trip, all business no pleasure."
When the beast spoke no lips could be seen to move but everyone could hear him. Dark mysterious smoke moved from within the dark hood where the red eye was.

To his men, "Spread out, they are here somewhere."
The warriors moved out searching the parked vessels. They also began to surround the club. Coming out of the large sub behind Blav were two creatures known as Vronexs that better resembled giant Arachnids than men. They walked on four exoskeleton legs that came from underneath very long insect abdomens. The creatures abdomen then curved and turned up. Then mounted to the abdomen was a massive head. The Vronexs had a humanoid like face with sharp teeth and an armored skull like a rhino. Attached to the upper abdomen were two appendages that had joints like elbows but instead of hands each had a single long claws that were as long as swords. When they moved their armored exoskeleton clicked and vibrated through the water.

Atop the club, Demetris felt something ever so slight with their arrival. The manatee man grabbed his cup. He put his lips over the cover and an opening formed. He sucked the whole drink, creature and all. Moon was frozen at the sight.

Then to Moon, "Are you going to drink your sunrise?"

She slid it to him, "All yours buddy."

He slurped it up too. Demetris handed the man a small pouch. The man opened it and Moon saw within the pouch were small sea shells. They were bright silver but also very shiny and reflected off the full light spectrum in the form of rainbows. Pretty she thought.

At the back entrance to the club a squad of Dacacians filled the club and started making their way along the perimeter of the dance floor. Blav entered but made his way around the opposite side of the pyramid from where Moon and Demetris were. Blav moved in the shadows and even appeared cloaked as he moved. As he made it around to the lower front he saw the manatee man leaving from Demetris and Moon's table.

Demetris stood cautiously, "We got what we came for and it's time to go."

Demetris was now moving fast. He pulled slightly on Moon's arm and they made it to the platform. But then he saw the Dacacians on the lower level. Demetris looked at the front entrance and Dacacian Guards were screening everyone that tried to leave. Right as they stepped off the lift at the bottom level a sharp powerful claw came down toward Demetris head and at the last minute he moved and it crashed into the pillar behind him. Even as Demetris was drawing his swords another spiked claw came down just barely missing him again. Moon fell but then was crawling away below the pounding of the arachnids heavy spiked paws. Demetris fought with speed and violence striking and blocking blow after blow. Both Vronexs were moving and striking at him. As Demetris moved and fought some of his blue energy that he had cast to Moon started flowing back in a small but visible particle stream. Moon did not notice it until she started to float up off the floor. Then she saw it and realized what it meant. Soon she would not be able to breathe and most likely be crushed. She pushed the button in her suit. Out of the tube a line of energy formed over her mouth and nose. She started swimming panicky toward the front of the club.

Strike, Strike, dodge, dash, strike, strike, stab.

The battle surged on, left hand blocked the Vronex claw on the left, right hand blocked on the right. The Vronex on the right tried to encircle him and come from behind. Demetris threw his right sword and it struck with force right into its head between its eyes. But the beast swatted it away. Throwing his sword freed his right hand for his gun. He pulled the heavy barreled gun and let it loose on the beast landing shots to the head, throat, and abdomen dropping it. Then he turned on the left dodging and fighting the other beast's claws with his sword. One of the claws got through striking Demetris right in the left shoulder. He swung with his blade and sliced at the beast's throat opening it up. The beast fell heavy but its claw was still attached to his shoulder pinning him to the wall.

Moon was swimming as fast as she could. She was struggling to survive. She made it to the entrance port of the Air lounge. She spun the handle and made it into the chamber. The water drained quickly and pressurized. She fell to the floor.

In the darkness of the club Blav appeared to be gestating something within his dark hood. Then a seam opened and unfolded like a large oversized coat. From within the deep darkness of the cloak a white creature was moving. And then suddenly stepping out of the darkness a beautiful blonde human female in an all-white body suit stepped out. Blav then closed the hood and again retreated into the shadows and disappeared.

Demetris pulled the massive claw with force and released it from his shoulder and the dead beast dropped. He was panicked and upset looking for Moon. He made his way through the club.

The DJ then said into the speaker, "Battle to the swordsman!"
The club patrons yelled in excitement and everyone started getting back to surrounding the pyramid as he turned on the next set of beats.

Inside the Air Lounge the young blond woman reached down to Moon and helped her up.

"You ok hon?"

"I think so."

"How about I treat you to a soda?"

The woman was really striking. And she had a southern accent that reminded Moon of the beach grounders. They sat at the counter and the squidbot took their order and retrieved it from inside itself delivering it up.

Demetris noticed that the Dacacians near the front started to pull back. He made his way back to the front, wounded holding his shoulder.

"I'm Isabella Wright."

Moon still exhausted from her swim, "Oh thank you for your help."

"My my what was all that mess about?"

"I don't really know."

Moon then realizing how out of place the woman looked. Even the other humans in the air lounge all looked weathered and sea soaked. But she looked so put together. Even her hair was styled.

"What are you doing here?" Moon asked.

"Well it really is the same old story. Damsel in distress. I was on an aerial transport that crashed into the sea. I somehow made it to an island on a life boat. I was there all by my lonesome for years. Then some nice smugglers were on a trip to here and next thing you know I've been in Anchali for..um..almost four years now.

Oh how I would love to get back to New Atlanta."
Then as if Moon had forgot about Demetris until this very moment; she began to look around and stood up.

"I've got to check on my friend."

"You mean the handsome man coming in the chamber as we speak."
Demetris came in and although he noticed Isabella he didn't say anything to her.

But to Moon, "We've got to leave."
In his weakened state he bumped into a particularly gnarly patron as he and Moon moved toward the exit chamber. Demetris began to move his hand in patterns and the blue energy formed over his wrist.

Then to his wrist, "Nerwin I need you to meet us at the Air Lounge immediately."
The man he bumped stood up. He was long, skinny and rugged. His skin looked strangely weathered almost like human leather with scars and botches everywhere. He wore no shirt but had on pants and boots that looked like they were made from shark skin. Over his head was a gold metal diving helmet. It was shaped and permanently formed over his head and went over portions of his chest and back. As he stood he pulled out a long sword that looked like it had been scavenged from some long lost pirate ship. Whether man or beast it was not clear the helmet hid his face. He launched at Demetris from behind.

Moon saw it, "Watch out!"

Demetris ducked and dove pushing Moon out of the way. The man brought down a heavy boot right on Demetris' injured shoulder. Demetris already tired from his previous battle was doing everything he could to block and move out of the way of the sharp but rusted sword. Moon was trapped underneath and behind him against the wall and the floor.

"You Luas think you own this place."

'Swoosh'

"We have been here as long as you."

'Swoosh'

Demetris wasn't sure how much longer he could defend himself. He tried to retrieve his swords or his gun but they were pinned between him and the floor and Moon. He kept trying to grab at the man's hand. He was using his heavy bracers on his forearms to block the swords blows. The man came down on Demetris and put his knee over his left arm and then grabbed his right. Demetris was defenseless. The crooked man raised his sword and just as he began to come down on both of them in slow motion a white energy formed like sparks on the surface of his helmet then it formed a circle expanding outward faster and faster until it caught up to real time and exploded through the helmet like a bolt of lightning completely frying the man's head within the helmet. Then he collapse and fell on Demetris. Demetris and Moon both worked together to force the large man off of them. Isabella was there helping dig them out too. They both saw it at the same time. She had a B74 energy weapon still in her hand. She quickly holstered it on her side like a real legit sea cowgirl. Then they all stood.

"You saved us" announced Moon.
She gave her a big warm hug. Demetris wasn't so trusting. Right then Nerwin came through the air lock.

"I'm here, I'm here."

"Where were you when we needed you?" Demetris walked past him.

Moon looked at Isabella, "Do you want to come with us?"

Isabella looked shyly toward Demetris, "Really back to New Atlanta."

Demetris quickly dismissive, "No, no, no, no time and no room."

Moon gave him a big puppy dog look, "But she saved us it's the least we can do."

Demetris stepped up to her, "Who are you exactly?"

She looked deep into his eyes and with a hint of girlish charm, "I'm just a girl looking for a ride." At this close, her eyes were the most unique all white with no pupils. But there was a slight hue of red around the ring of where the pupil might have been. Demetris should have known at that moment something was off but he missed it. Through her eyes it led back to Blav. And we can now see him looking through the eyes of his puppet.

Nerwin opened up a back portal near the side of his cast iron belly. Moon scrunched in and sat on a small seat attached to his insides. Isabella hit several buttons on her suit and a thin shield came up over her whole body. The three of them made their way as fast as they could to the Cheonia.

Back on the ship Demetris undocked and made his way back out on the street they came in on. Moon crawled out of Nerwin.

"Thanks Nerwin."

"Oh you are welcome Moon. I hope it wasn't too cramped. My last upgrade added a ship to land multiplexer and a counter electronic beacon system."

She laughed uncomfortably as she realized she was inside a living and thinking creature.

"No it was fine."

Demetris caught something, "Wait what did you say?"

Nerwin repeated robotically, "I was wondering if there was enough room for Mo..."

"No not that, about the upgrades."

Before Nerwin could answer it hit Demetris. He used the Plava Boya to adjust some controls and put the ship on autopilot. Then got up and approached Moon in the galley. She was drying off some of the water that got through the energy field. Isabella was there too.

"What on earth are you talking about?" Nerwin asked playfully.

Demetris went straight to Moon, "Let me see your arm."

She rolled up her sleeve showing her PDS.

"Who are you?"

She playfully looked at Isabella, "I'm just a girl trying to get back to my boyfriend."

The girls got the joke but Demetris missed it.

"Nerwin initiated a med pod."

"What procedure are we doing today Skipper?"

Moon confused as he held her arm, "Wait, procedure. What's going on?"

Isabella stepped up, "What are we doing?"

"That's how they found us. It's your PDS. Who are you?"

This time he wasn't joking around, "What is your name?"

"Moon Cadel."

Then he realized the multitude of trouble they were in, "As in the daughter of Lord Cadel?"

Nerwin was at a control panel in the galley and a side door opened, the table and chairs moved and went away into a compartment as a medical pod with a dentist looking chair emerged.

"Well we got the dark ones tracking us most likely because of Hanno."

"Dark Ones who are they." Both women asked.

"Only the most dangerous military arm from one of the ruling nobles from my home planet."

DANIEL J. NESHER

The pod opened and Demetris led Moon by holding her hands and helping her to a seat.

"And now we probably have every intelligence officer of the Order looking for us too." As soon as she sat, straps grabbed and secured both her arms and the pod closed securing her inside.

Nerwin asked, "What procedure sir?"

"Remove Moon's PDS on her right wrist."

Nerwin then asked for clarification, "Remove her right wrist, copy that."
When Moon herd him say that she got a look of terror. Demetris held his hand out and smiled slightly embarrassed.

"Its fine I got it."
He moved Nerwin out of the way and then entered the procedure. Before she could protest she was instantly knocked out. Several automated arms and blue energy went to work cutting, removing, and then repairing at the Nano level Moon's wrist.
The pod began to open and she came to just as quick as she passed out.

"My wrist I need my.."
She lifted her hand and it was fine. They all laughed and looked at Nerwin. But when Isabella looked on from behind them her sweet charming face changed to a strange intense face.

CHAPTER 11: THREE MEN FROM THE EAST

The Cheonia rose up from out of the depths. On the ships virtual screens the Chesapeake Bridge and tunnel were under water and completely destroyed and laid to ruin. Demetris was navigating a route between the rubble under water. They passed Cape Charles and made their way up the Chesapeake Bay. Due to the past nuclear war, ice melt, and climate change the whole eastern seaboard had changed. It was much warmer and the sea level had risen hundreds of feet inland. Under New Atlanta the water cycle was interrupted and captured by the city. But here near where old Washington DC used to be, was a deluge. The ship still powered through underwater but from the air above, rich water soaked mangrove forests dominated the landscape. There were deep wide water trenches that crawled out in every direction. Many of the water ways were deeper and wider than the

Amazon River.   No longer was there flat grass lands or city and highways.   The Land was long gone and buried under the sea.   As the Cheonia got farther inland, Demetris had to move and search through the waterways like trying to find his way through a maze.   Far behind them just out of sensor range, from the sky something could be seen hunting them.   It was long and huge and moved through the winding waterways with ease. As it moved around a corner several hundred meters behind the ship, portions of its body could be seen moving at the water's surface.   It was a huge snake like beast with a head as big as the ship. Each turn and each move the ship made, the beast followed patiently behind waiting for the right opportunity.

Deep underwater in a large beautiful space was a large circular bowl the size of a stadium. It looked like it had been formed naturally but it was not.   It was the direct result of a mega nuclear ground strike.   The crater over several millennia had changed and was now full of rich sea life. The whole area formed the most beautiful Coral Reef. More beautiful than you might see in the Polynesian Islands.   There were sharp colors of green, red, purple, yellow, and blue.   But also a mixture of all the colors in between. Filled with rich sea life swimming and living abundantly. A pod of dolphins jumped the surface of the water and made their way deep along the reef's edge. Then as if in a relay race we are handed off to a large sea turtle who swims even deeper down the reef's moving living edge. A dark blue star fish moves over the coral below him as the turtle glides downward. Off in the distance on the far edge of the reef a small portion of the Washington Monument was barely visible. It had coral growing up the sides and was tilted at a strange angle. Down at the basin of the bowl was a newer structure made out of stone. It rose up from the seafloor directly in the middle of the bowl. It was a mixture of old and new with rocks forming a large circle with an opening in the center. On a rock platform at the center and bottom of the reef was a lone woman. She was wearing a two piece swimsuit but not the kind you would think of today. It was connected to other parts of her apparel. Part of the suit led up to her shoulder and forearm bracers. And parts of her bottoms led down and formed and connected to armor. She was barefoot but also had some sort of armor sandal that covered the top of her foot and her shin. She was sitting in a Lotus position with her legs crossed. She had bright blue hair with long braids on each side of her head and a long pony tail in the back. Her hair was moving magically in the ocean around her. She was forming and moving her hands and fingers in some sort of ancient mystical art. As she moved and formed, the Plava Boya formed and moved with her hands. Streams of the energy filled her body and marked her with stripes and lines as beautiful tattoos along her arms, legs, and torso revealed themselves. The energy glowed and formed characters, signs, and symbols in front of her and all around her. And she moved the characters around like a martial artists might move a weapon or a dancer might move their body. She started to float up off the floor of the ocean. The energy formed and grew out of her. The rocks in the structure behind her filled with the energy and began to move and separate into their building blocks with the blue energy between each block. The sea life began to move and respond to the energy too. Several dolphins saw it and played around in it as it grew up and filled up the whole bowl. Then the water moved and swirled and formed with the energy. Then suddenly she cut her head to the East.

The lone woman known as Deyva then said, "The devil comes in the face of a friend!"
She switched and punched her hands in a martial arts move towards the East.

Back at the Cheonia, Demetris and Moon were in the two front seats and Isabella was in one of the back seats. The blue energy from Deyva moved across the ocean and into their vessel. It burst past and through the ship and landed in the chest of Isabella. She was blasted backwards and also through the ship and like a ghost disappeared.

Somewhere deep in the center of the ocean in Baron Blav's dark mysterious ship, Isabella suddenly appeared as if she had been thrust through time and space itself. She landed on her back at the feet of Blav. He was surprised but then she just stood in front of him. He then opened up his body but also his cloak. She now appeared more animal like than human and crawled back into him and then the dark front closed.

Moon fearfully asked, "What was that? What happened to Isabella?"

Demetris just said, "That was interesting." Behind the Cheonia the long sleek beast started closing the distance. The Cheonia turned left then right and the speed of the beast could be seen with the change in the movement of the water on the surface. Now it was right behind them and its massive head started clearing the water's surface. Its head looked more like a giant lizard than snake with razor sharp teeth shinning out of its huge mouth. The top of its head breached the surface right as the Cheonia approached the entrance to the reef. It now surged forward opening its mouth wide enough to completely consume the small vessel.

Inside the Cheonia the beauty of the bowl reef came into view. Demetris and Moon were completely unaware of the imminent threat behind them. Their front one eighty view was bright with all the colors and sights ahead. It wasn't until a proximity alert sounded that they turned and looked at the back view. All they could see was mouth and teeth. Demetris still hurting from his last two battles, grabbed the controls that were controlled by the blue energy out of his hands and thrusted the ship forward as fast as he could. While turning and also trying to shield the ship with his remaining energy. The jaws came down on the back half of the ship and landed on his energy shield. Demetris felt the impact within his body as if he had been bitten himself. It caused the ship to get caught in the beast's mouth and Moon went flying forward from the change in velocity. She crashed down into the lower area of the control panel with her legs and feet over her head. Demetris tried to push again. Then suddenly a great wave of blue energy struck the beast in the face and eyes. Like shots out of an energy cannon. Blast after blast hit it. The ship then started to move. Then they saw it. It was Deyva floating in front of the ship on the edge of the bowl with her arms outstretched and her braids energized behind her. And then she gathered her strength and did one more finger, hand, arm movement and shot another at the beast. It struck hard and the beast let go. Then Demetris saw her on his screens but also connected with her through the Plava Boya.

"What a sight for sore eyes." He said with a huge smile.

"You're not too bad looking either." She said. Moon didn't hear them but saw their faces, "Who's this, your girlfriend?"

Teenagers he thought. As they followed her into the bowl, dolphins swam in front of her and somewhere in the middle of the reef, Moon's eyes got ten times bigger.

"Oooo look Demetris."

Two beautiful blue whales swam from each side of the bowl and cross in front of Deyva as if to say goodbye. She ran her hand along one and saw into his very personal eye. Then the whales crossed and both jumped the water at the same time. Then swam out of the bowl and out to sea. Demetris pulled his ship into a spot near the building at the base of the bowl. They exited out of the ship and Demetris had healed enough to support Moon with his energy again so she didn't have to ride in Nerwin. Moon's eyes were wide open. A sea turtle swam to her. She grabbed some sea grass and fed him like giving a dog a cookie bone. He smiled wide and then swam away.

Deyva approached them and instantly went in and gave Demetris a huge hug.

"Where have you been? It's been too long."

He arched back from the hug holding her shoulders with his hands, "I've found Hanno."

She changed from happiness to seriousness, "Where?"

"Well he was at the beach near New Atlanta but now he's at a place called Oasis."

Deyva's face filled with worry. Then she noticed the sweet young Moon.

She smiled again, "Well who is this young human?"

Moon was half walking but half swimming and came right up to her. She gave her a big hug and

Deyva reciprocated.

"I'm Moon, and um I think Hanno's girlfriend."

Deyva looked at Demetris as if asking without asking, 'Is he old enough for that sort of thing."

Then back to Moon, "Of course you are, look how pretty you are."

Hanno was standing near a small group that had formed near the side of the water tower. A number of guards stood by. Granger and Jerry arrived with several other guards.

"Oh my sweet pilgrims thank you for volunteering for this very important duty."

Hanno was looking like he was not feeling well. His skin had turned ashy and he was looking like he was drying up.

Granger continued, "You carry hope with you. You are the disciples I send into the world with a message of good news."

Each formed in a line near Granger who had made his way to the port door on the side of the tower. He entered a code into a cypher lock and the door swung open. Two guards entered first and started making their way up the metal ladder that went up to New Atlanta. Then one by one the volunteers stepped up to Granger. He handed them a very old and very small Gideon's Bible. Then Jerry put on each, a small smart watch he had developed.

Jerry said robotically every time, "Here is your passport and credentials. Cover it up and

don't take off."
It was a device to spoof the PDS monitoring system of the Order.

Hanno stepped up to Granger, "When can I go up?"

Granger talking in between hugs and well wishes to the pilgrims, "Soon Hanno, soon."

"Well if I don't go soon, I'm going to have to go back to the beach."

Granger stepped aside so the others couldn't hear, "We talked about this. We need to test the passage and see how exposed we are to the eyes of the order."

A lone guard sat atop of the wall on the Eastern gate of Oasis. On his right was a pipe with an electronic sensor that looked out into the desert. On his left a mounted fifty caliber machine gun. No one ever came from the East. It was the most deserted. Those who came to Oasis always came from the South. It was closest to the workable roads. And it was known that all must first pass through the visitor's center and the market, before being granted access to the area on the North and East side. He was a young man with a leather vest and pants wearing an old school baseball hat on backwards. He had his feet up and just rested a sandwich on his stomach. He laid out his napkins on his chest. His glass of water within reach to his left and some dried banana chips to his right. He lifted the sandwich to his mouth.

'Beep, Beep, Beep, sensor data indicates

perimeter alarm.'

Oasis's last attack was twenty five years ago from a raider village to the West. But this guard hadn't even born then. He had never seen war. He paused in frustration. He looked out into the desert and saw nothing. He kicked the sensor with his boot and went back to his lunch.

'Beep, Beep, Beep, sensor data indicates perimeter alarm.'

This time it came after a big bite.

"Damn it!" He said with a full mouth.

He spilled everywhere. He sat up again. From behind him, his senior officer came up a set of stairs. He had on binoculars and searched the desert. When the junior guard saw him he stood. On the far edge of the desert, three men on foot approached. He searched around them and behind them. There were no vehicles and no other threats.

"Ahhh it's just wanders." The senior belted.

"Tell them to go to the Southern gate."

The senior guard left as the mysterious men slowly walked up to the Eastern Gate. As they slowly approached the young guard finished his sandwich and chips and drank a long cool drink of his water. Now three men in their forties were down right in front of his gate. They wore similar dress to those in New Atlanta. Formal retro suits with ties and tails. But there was something that looked different. The suits almost looked like they were on top of something. They were obviously very lean and muscular. Then he first noticed they had on PDS's on their wrist. A clear violation and enough to get them denied access. But then under their suits was some sort of security armor.

He spoke with courage from his protected position up on the wall, "Hey stop right there."
They did. The man in the middle had thick black hair combed back. He had a large thick black mustache that ran down to his chin on both sides of his mouth. And when he spoke, he spoke with a devilish grin.

"Hello, my name is Leon Pavlovich. What is your name young man?"

"It doesn't matter what my name is. You are not welcome here."
He tried to sound tough but Pavlovich was un-phased.

"Do you have someone that is charge that can come talk to me?"

"No one has time for you. Go away."
Pavlovich looked along the wall and took in his surroundings. He then pulled up something on his PDS. The tower was just on the other side of the gate and it appeared Pavlovich knew that.

Pavlovich then said, "Hey whatever you think you are doing with the tower, you don't know what you are doing?"
The young guard might have been naive but he wasn't dumb. He motioned to the senior guard who was joking around with several other guards within the wall. He was upset at being pulled

away. He rushed up the steps.

"Hey dude if you don't leave this gate right now you will be wasted."
Several of the other guards were starting to pay attention too. The young guard grabbed the machine gun near him. Several of the guards started showing up on the wall with automatic rifles that were a mix between old ballistic and new energy weapons. Pavlovich and his men didn't even seem to care.

Pavlovich just increased his grin like he was happy at their response, "Are you sure you don't want to talk about this like adults?"

The senior guard sent a runner to Granger. Granger turned and started heading toward the wall. Jerry seeing the increase in energy also made his way calculating and creating math formulas at the activity. Granger stepped up next to the senior guard. He paused to take in the three. He observed their clothing and their PDS's. Then he searched the perimeter looking for more Order troops or vehicles. He saw none.

"Who are you?" he asked.

"I am Leon Pavlovich, Granger I assume."
He didn't like that, Pavlovich already knew his name.

"Yes if you are from the Order, we have a peace treaty and your being here is in direct…"

Before he could finish Leon interrupted, "You know why we are here."
Then he finished with his horrible sarcastic grin.

"What have you been up to Granger?"

"Nothing involving The Order's business."

"That's not exactly true. What's going on with the Tower?"

They knew he thought.

Inside the tower the last set of guards and pilgrims had made it to the top. At the top a door in the roof opened up into a small mechanical room in the basement of a building. And then they had another set of ten rungs up. One of the guards went up first. The ladder led to an old panel and door. He forced open the door and it opened into a lower floor inside an old reunion station in the heart of New Atlanta. A tactical team was waiting for them and pounced. The guards were shot with energy weapons instantly and the pilgrims were taken into custody. Then a mecha robot rolled over to the door and started using an energy tool to create a thick metallic cap over the door.

Pavlovich grinned and then just said, "There has to be an example made."

With that he raised his right hand and index finger and just circled it in the air. Before any of the Oasis guards could pull up their weapons; high above out of the bottom of New Atlanta, huge artillery guns came to life and turned and adjusted out of the bottom. Large sections once thought to be a part of the cities mechanical and utility systems were now clearly seen as a military defense.

'Boom boom boom boom!'

Rounds of bright red and orange balls exploded

out of the artillery heading right at the east wall and the grounds around the tower. Granger was thrown far but missed by a round that killed the young guard. The Eastern gate was completely obliterated and laid open.

"Well boys looks like daddy opened the door." Pavlovich said with a grin.

Hanno was so distracted by the conversation with Granger he didn't even noticed what was going on until the fireballs where raining down on them. Now he was running and dodging as they exploded all around him.

'Boom, boom, boom, boom!'

He dashed and ran. One close explosion exploded on him but he instinctually protected himself with his Boya energy shield. But the blast knocked him into the dry well at the center of the court yard. Jerry was still up on the portion of wall that was not blown up. He was moving his hands excitedly seeing the fireworks as a great physics problem he was witnessing, completely unware of the danger. Hanno ran to him. A rope had bust loose from a canvas tent. Hanno launched on the rope and his energy pushed him up and around the corner of a building. As he his right foot separated into three tentacles that grabbed and grappled him through the buildings beams, awnings, and pipes flipping him high and then he landed right at Jerry and grabbed him. Then was off again now using both sets of tentacles to flip and move along the wall. He moved around two other buildings as they fell all around them. And not a moment too soon as a fireball exploded right where Jerry was standing.

Pavlovich and his two men pulled from holsters behind their backs short energy rifles. They moved in a line shooting with great accuracy anyone in their path. As they rounded the entrance, the one on the right turned and targeted Hanno, Jerry, and a little girl. Hanno transformed and surround all three of them with his tentacles but also his shield. The shots bounced off. Then he transformed back. A man rushed up and grabbed the girl and Hanno and Jerry made their way to the Northern side of the wall.

'Boom, boom, boom!'
The three attackers were protected by the artillery above and anyone who came close was pin point struck with explosions.

Jerry showed Hanno a small door that let them through the wall out into the desert. Hanno saw Granger moving under some debris near the devastation at the east gate. They both made their way to him. Pavlovich saw them and turned toward the gate and their position. He shoulder mounted his weapon. Hanno was at Granger and lifted the debris off of him. Jerry was helping too but was so distracted by all the activity.

Then Jerry said, "Shoulder mounted Safko Dealan energy rifle. The effective rifle used by intelligence officers of the Order has multiple attack options. At stun phase it will deliver 10 milliamperes to paralyze all of the subject's muscles and cause incredibly painful spasms."

Hanno was barely listening to him trying to lift a beam that was trapping Granger.

"Jerry help me!"

Jerry helped lift but was still dialoging, "At Kill setting the rifle can release 10,000 milliamps and destroy its target. It has a combat range of 450 meters."

They moved the debris and helped Granger to stand.

"We are at 350 meters and will surely be..." A blast from Pavlovich's rifle struck Jerry right in the chest blowing him free. Then a second shot hit Granger as he tried to duck hitting him square in the ribs. Hanno caught him and was holding him. The third shot lined up and exploded but bounced of a blue energy field around them. Hanno didn't know what was happening. Another shot burst and exploded on the shield. Pavlovich started moving in their direction firing more and more shots. Hanno looked behind him and at first saw Moon. Her hair from constantly immersion in the Plava Boya had changed from blond to all white. She was sitting on some sort of flying bike. She had her white hair in a ponytail. She had on a black jacket that was cropped and showing her cute belly. She had on black shorts and long black boots. Over her sleeves and boots where bracers and armor. The whole bike was energized by the Plava Boya. Next to her was Demetris who had a similar bike but it had an elevated passenger seat that went up a level behind him. Deyva was riding on the back part of Demetris bike. She was forming a shield that was protecting Hanno.

Granger in his last breath, "Hanno remember that God loves you. And let no man keep you from being free."

With that he pulled from his coat a complete bible. It was in a hard bound cover with a lock on it. He then pulled from around his neck a necklace with a cross and the key to the bible. And with that the founder and leader of the Oasis died in his arms.

"Hanno come on we need to go."

Up far above in a floating command base. Lord Cadel and Detective Denton watched the battle on multiple screens. When both of them saw Moon you could see it in their faces.

Lord Cadel yelled out, "Halt all artillery!"

Denton was relaying to the communicator who was relaying to the three ground officers.

"Halt all attacks, wanted missing juvenile has been spotted."

They repeated it multiple times but none of the men could see what they were talking about. They were all looking at the Oasis survivors and didn't even consider the three that just pulled up.

Hanno jumped on behind Moon and grabbed her around the waist. The two bikes took off with a blast.

"Denton do something!" Shouted Cadel.

With one swift move, Denton ran to the side panel and swiped his PDS and then hit a code into a display. Suddenly a door opened up to some sort of tube. He jumped in, and as soon as his whole body was in the tube, the panel door closed and the floor opened. He was dropped but also guided by several sets of energy lasers. They dropped him from the high command center straight down into a ground level building. The building was two stories and appeared to be some sort of municipal building. Several citizens on the sidewalks saw him and wondered what was going on. A portion of the roof opened and he then was guided through the building and down into the basement. The lasers guided him further dropping him into a ship built into the basement of the building. The ship then from the underside of New Atlanta came to life and broke free of the city and quickly dropped into the sky headed to the ground.

Pavlovich ran up, "About damn time Detective."
The three hoped in and then made pursuit toward the two bikes across the desert.

CHAPTER 12:
HERO TWINS

Two futuristic bikes made it away quickly from the Oasis heading northeast towards the shore. The bikes floated powered by the Plava Boya. Somewhere near the Pamlico River, the bikes dove underwater into the river. The bikes then pulled into the bottom of the load chamber of the Cheonia. Demetris quickly made his way to the helm and powered up and took off down the river heading for the open ocean.

Denton's ship pulled up to an abandoned bridge overlooking the Pamlico River. The top of the ship retracted and he walked out on top of the ship. He stood looking out over the barren land and river. Back over his shoulders was New Atlanta. From this view it was massive and covered everything in the sky behind him even though he was several miles away from the cities edge.

"Command any site on where the bikes went."

"No Denton. The bikes had some sort of

DANIEL J. NESHER

cloaking. We lost them the moment they got out from under the city."
We see Denton's face as he looks out over the sea and wilderness.

Back at the protected reef a Giant Manta Ray glided over the reef. It crossed the reef to the circular stones at the entrance to the circular opening in the middle. If you were to enter in the opening a hidden structure would reveal itself. The walls all aligned vertically one to another running inward in a circular shape but open above to the sea. In the inner corridor a number of Luas were working and moving. On the left were rows of open walls twenty feet high open to the reef. On the right another circular wall built in and enclosed with floor to ceiling doors. A particular uniquely looking red Lua was pushing a large cart as she floated in the sea within the building. She went through a large opening on the right side that was in the shape of an oval. Along the whole opening were carvings and designs in the mantle. She stopped at the end of the hall and then started to float up. As she floated up her bottom half transformed and her long red tentacles come to life where her legs were, but also from out of her back and the back of her head. She was full of tentacles and she was very beautiful and elegant. She had red and white stripes that ran the length of her tentacles but also all over her chest, arms and face. She appeared to dance as she moved and went up ten stories. At the top she came to a landing and then transformed back. She pushed the tray and appeared to walk and float across a marble floor. She came out of a corridor onto a beautiful opening. Built into the side of the coral reef was a balcony. From far away it was completely camouflaged in the reef. But here up close, it was bright green with yellow and blue markings and clearly man or rather Lua made. The opening in which the red Lua came out of, had a statue carved into the reef over the opening. It was of an ancient past female Lua of renown. The balcony could now be seen as more of a tall tower that reached all the way up from the right of the circular opening on bottom entrance. On the balcony were several tables. Nerwin met the red Lua at the cart and they both served the food to the tables. Demetris, Moon, Hanno, and Deyva were present. But also several other Luas.

Nerwin handed Moon her plate, "I thought shrimp and lobster would be something you might like."

"Oh thank you Nerwin, you are so sweet."
When she looked at her plate the shrimp and lobster were still swimming in their containment plates. There was also some seaweed, kelp, and something that looked like moss. She ate those first. Hanno sitting next to her dug in as if he hadn't eaten in a long time. He grabbed a handful of shrimp and chomped them live. Then broke the lobster in two and started eating it shell and all.

Deyva sitting next to Moon reached over and

leaned in, "Want help?"

"Please thanks."

Moon watched as Deyva killed, cleaned and shelled the lobster. Then heated it with a torch device near her plate.

"My little nephew likes them prepared this way."

Moon tried it and minus the butter, it was as good as any she had eaten on the surface. As the guests began to finish their food, Nerwin and the red Lua brought desert. Everyone was served a strange dark material under an opaque air bubble. It looked like something that might have come out of a dolphin's butt.

"What's this?" asked Moon.

Deyva leaned in, "Chocolate brownies, where not monsters after all."

She smiled funny and then popped the bubble and before the sea could dissolve it away, she ate it in several bites. Moon followed and when she tasted the chocolate, while under the Plava Boya, the combination of sweet, chocolate, and sea salt was the most satisfying she has ever tasted. The whole group saw her reaction and instant laughter broke out. When Hanno saw it, he gave her another type of smile and then reached under the table and held her hand. Moon had been changing in many ways while being under the Plava Boya. First her hair changed from blond to white with ever so slight streaks of blue. But also her skin and body were changing. Now under the table we could see she was barefoot. Her feet had grown slightly longer but also there were webs starting to form between her toes. Hanno moved a tentacle from the back of his calf. At first we can see the suckers and hooks of his tentacles. But then he made them disappear and his tentacle was as smooth and soft as skin. He wrapped it around her legs and feet. And it was the most sensual feeling she had ever had.

Demetris asked Hanno, "Is it true that you don't remember your past?"

"Well I have flashes but yes it's like I was born on the beach three years ago after landing on the shore in front of the Salty Tallywhacker."

"Is Hanno a Lua?" Moon held his hand in both her hands.

Demetris and Deyva looked at each other, "Yes and no."

Demetris tried to explain, "Luas came to your earth three thousand years ago. It was an accident and a blessing. We come from a world called Syrena. A bidaiari ship..." Looking at Deyva "How do you say bidaiari?"

Deyva answered, "Passenger ship."

Demetris continued, "Yes there was three thousand Luas on a Passenger Ship and we hit an Actueel Trenuto."

He looked at Deyva but answered for himself, "Storm or rather Hurricane."

She corrected him, "Underwater Hurricane."

"The storm was horrible. I was the ship's religious director."

Deyva added, "Um Chaplin."

"Yes Chaplin. Syrena is a water planet. The only land that exists is under its seas. The storm led us into what we thought was a whirlpool. As our ship went down it then felt like it changed directions and went up."

The group was enthralled with the story. Especially Hanno and Moon who were hearing it for the first time.

"The whirlpool inverted and turned into a cyclone that stretched into the sky and beyond. Time stood still and then we crashed down back into the sea. Our ship was damaged so we thought that explained the sensor malfunctions. The water temperature and currents were all off. We looked for our home port of Pliev but kept getting lost. None of the geography seemed right."

Deyva leaned into to Moon, "He means the seafloor geography?"

Demetris continued, "Then we found the seafloor rising up out of the sea. We had never seen dryland before so we investigated. We found two islands which we later learned were Reunion and Mauritius off the coast of Madagascar. And we found you, humans. This was three thousand years ago. It was after your first global nuclear war. These two small islands had survived and were doing the best they could. We had technology with the Plava Boya that could reproduce you're..." He paused to find the word. "Your biological needs, water, food, etc."

Deyva took over, "You have to understand our religion led us to believe that we were the only sentient creatures in the whole universe made by our creator. We were the Sons of Atlas. We were God's special children. And now to find a whole new species."

It was like an old married couple telling their story in turns.

Demetris then took over, "We have always been able to manipulate and adapt our bodies to whatever environment was before us. And we quickly adapted and formed bodies to match yours. It took a while to learn your language but our technology helped. We brought the Plava Boya to the humans. And they used it to build their cities and their weapons."

Moon going back to the question of religion, "I used to ask my friend who was a Christian, 'Could God have created other planets with other creatures?' He would say, "Of course He could, but if He did, He is still the God of all the Universe and would reveal himself to them as well."

Hanno added, "It sounds like He did."

Nerwin and Tellua, the red Lua, had cleared the tables. Deyva led them in through the opening and then to another study within the structure. The study had high ceilings like that of a great chapel with pillars that reached up from the floor to the ceiling. But it was also a long narrow cylinder space. At several levels within the study it was very homey. There were chairs, hammocks, and other seating options; some floor level, some at points mid and high in the room. Tellua went up to the center of the room but also mid-way up the height of the room. She formed her tentacles from her side and swiped her hooks on her tentacles and they made flashes of light. The flashes almost appeared as sparks in the water but were something else. Then in the center before her was a receptacle made out of stone that had stone around the center both horizontally and vertically. In the middle of the stone structure were white crystals. When her flashes hit the crystals the crystals came to life. And then there was bright blue and red coming off the crystals and also heat. It was a fire place under water with blue flames going upward and downward heating the whole room. The fireplace also had uniquely carved openings in the stone sending heat and light in all direction in the room. Moon jumped into a floating love seat and grabbed Hanno to sit with her. It was mid-way up near the fire. The other's entered the room and found their places. Some just floated near the fire and others sat.

Moon asked, "So who is Hanno?"
She was right to the point.

Deyva moved toward the wall across from her as Demetris sat to the side of Hanno and Moon.

Demetris then said, "Well after several hundred years on this planet we all settled in. We were stuck with no way to return to our home."
Deyva with her back to them.

She was preparing something while she talk, "Then when The Order took over, Luas were cast out of the cities. Many of us fled to the small human settlements across the world that were surviving outside the cities. But also we started building a home for ourselves here under your seas."

Demetris added, "Deyva became a teacher."

Moon ever curious, "That's what I want to be, what kind of teacher?"

"A teacher of the special arts and the Plava Boya."

"And I became a trader and translator trying to maintain a bridge between the Luas and the humans. It was in this role that I learned your bible. It helped me find insight to both our faiths and understand one of our prophecies."

As if the stage was set, Deyva brought out into the center of the room something in her tentacles out of a protected case. She had to use four to hold it. It was almost three quarters the size of her body. It looked like she might have pulled it from the reef. It was multicolored with openings on all sides. Some of the structures on it looked like crystals with tubes and openings. Other shapes looked like sea shells and sea creature fossils with spiral patterns and star shapes; all very natural, all very unique. All of the crystals, shapes, patterns and openings were built onto the device and went in all directions. She set it a drift and it floated in front of the guests in the study.

"This is The Stygian Regolith. Every ship captain was entrusted with one. It's our bible."

Hanno asked, "You were the ship captain?"

Deyva somewhat sad, "I was the highest ranking member to survive. I was the ship Soturi, or um Ship Warrior Director."

This time Demetris helped her, "Security Director."

"Right Security Director."

Deyva turned to the devise, "Echo show us Opinberun 4 and Ilmutus 23 thru 27."

Lights formed from within the device as it floated and moved with the slight currents in the room. Moon and Hanna sat up and watched closely. Then a small creature came out of one of the openings. He was small maybe six inches long. He was blue with a long slim torso that went from his head to a fish like tail. He almost disappeared into the sea if you were not looking right at him. But then there was an even thinner membrane that formed around his torso like some sort of swimming outer membrane. He had two arms and two hands. His hands had four long, slender, fingers that were as long as his arms. The tips of his fingers were bright blue. His small little face was human looking but also Lua looking. But had no visible nose or ears. Out the top of his head grew small feeler type appendages that also had bright blue tips. He moved his body like a fish and swam right up to Deyva. He made a low sweet noise that moved the water and he then rubbed up against her hand and then stopped and looked at everyone in the room with bright wide eyes. He made a sweet face to Moon and then swam quickly back into the Regolith.

Deyva added, "Echo in English please."
He started moving in and out of holes so quickly it was hard to keep up with him. Hanno and Moon had gotten closer and at one point he came out the side and stopped in front of their faces and smiled at them. Then like a child playing hide and seek, he was gone. From his movements and also from his voice a unique set of tones and sounds could be heard. The sounds and tones then formed and moved the water around the device. Before their eyes the water moved and formed a three dimensional water screen. And a video played. It was of a very old Lua. His head was more squid shaped and less human like but clearly a Lua.

"I am Tanel the first. Greetings to the Sons of Atlas. May God's grace shine upon you? In that day God will allow his people to be whisked away on a great storm. They will be taken to a foreign land. The creatures of that land will love the sky rather than the sea. But be of good faith. I will send someone of the tribe of Daihbi. He will be of the sky and the sea. And written upon his chest will be the path to follow."

Hanno pulled his hand gently away from Moon's hand and looked under his shirt at his birthmark. Moon saw it and knew instantly what it meant.

The water video continued, "This is what the Lord, the God of Atlas, says: The days are coming when I will bring my people back and restore them to the land of their ancestors."

The video finished and then the little creature named Echo came out like an obedient pet and sat in front of Deyva. Deyva gave him a small treat and stroked his back with one finger. Then booped him on the head. He rubbed against her hand. He then swam quickly and stopped in front of Moon. He floated in front of her face smiling. She slowly put out her hand, palm up with fingers spread. He swam into her hand and held her thumb with both his hands still looking at her.

"He wants another treat." Deyva explained. Deyva gave Moon a very small treat to share with him. He ate it while sitting on her hand. Then rubbed against her palm and swam off into the Regolith.

Deyva to the guests in the room, "Leave us." Tellua, Nerwin, and the other guests left. Alone Moon, Hanno, Deyva, and Demetris were in the room. Deyva put away the Regolith and motioned for the others to join her at her desk. She had a stone desk built into the side of the study wall. It was near where she had brought out the Regolith. There were shelves of all sorts along the wall. Some above the desk and some below. The desk was built into the wall and stretched seven feet into the opening. It was circular with lots of devices attached to both the top and bottom sides. She sat in a chair that appeared to be held in position near the desk by the Plava Boya. Hanno and Moon floated on the other side of the desk from her. Demetris joined her floating at her side. Deyva sat in the chair but then suddenly she adjusted the chair and it flipped upside down so she could access the other side of the table. Moon and Hanno just sort of slowly floated down and saw her working upside down. Moon smiled a funny smile at Hanno and he smiled back. There were all sorts of instruments somehow attached to the bottom side of the desk. She would pick up one and separate it but then put it down. She was searching for something. She then found it. She grabbed it and then adjusted again flipping her chair upright. It looked like a scope attached to a handle.

To Hanno she asked, "Do you mind. Can I see your birth mark more closely?"
Hanno somewhat self-consciously took off his shirt. Of course Moon had missed seeing her man with his underwater bod and looked on with interest. Deyva almost floating up and over the desk brought up the scope as a doctor running a test on a patient. She scanned his birth mark and then the scope projected it out over the desk.

"You can put your shirt back on."
Moon just said, "Oh really so soon."
This projection of the birthmark was so much more rich and layered then when Granger and Jerry projected it with their human computer

controlled holographics. Clearly the patterns was meant for the sea. The circle of patterns and characters that have been seen before were there. The lines and connections clearly visible.

Demetris read the visible markings around left of the circle, "The Sons of Atlas will return to the land."

Then around the right, "Hanno the son of sky and sea."

Moon excited, "It's like the prophecy."
Deyva and Demetris shared a look.

Then along the bottom, "Two from one. One for the light and one for the dark."

Then Demetris was following the finely drawn designs and zooming in on the words that followed the inner layer with the lines connected to the lines, "And here is listed Hanno's lineage. It gives father to son going all the way back to Atlas. Amazing."

Deyva was too amazed, "Let me try something."
Deyva began to move and manipulate the image as it floated in front of her desk. Demetris had his note book out and his pen that clearly now could also right underwater.

"Try changing the humus and deflection."
She made some adjustments. The circle grew to a multi-layered globe.

"Dissect it and expand, then zoom in."
Deyva moved other adjustments and the design moved and came apart. Now it was like looking

into a living cell. There was a tightly packed nucleus. Moving complex parts within parts all moving and working together like an organic clock or a complicated puzzle.

"There's a lot there, I recognize parts from my cellular biology class but many I don't."

"Moon is right this has ribosomes and cytoplasm that looks like it is a part of a human host but also lysosome, cilia, and Golgi from a Lua."

"Deyva enhance these here that look like chromosomes."

Deyva enhanced and enlarged the section he was talking about.

"Look at this structure. It almost looks like a combination of Lua and human DNA. Look at the carbon and hydrogen bases. Take out the base pair connections."

She did and another design came into view.

Then Deyva and Demetris together, "Now let's zoom back out."

They did and more patterns emerge.

"What does that look like?"

Hanno tilting his head, "A connect the dots."

Deyva rotated it.

Demetris, "There is depth here."

They zoomed back some more and then slowly started to rotate it.

Moon blurted out, "That looks like the Mayan Hero Twins. In my ancient civilizations class we learned about the hero twins and how the twins that were entwined came out of a cave. One good and one evil. The location is supposed to be in La Venta a town off the coast of the gulf of New Mexico."

This clicked with something Demetris saw, "Deyva rotate ninety degrees to the right and hold."

"It's a living map." He shouted.

They didn't see it.

"Look here the outline of the twins lower half is the Gulf of Mexico. The first point on the 'connect the dots' must be near what I can only imagine is La Venta."

Now a global underwater map was coming into view. The points that started at the gulf led to points in the Atlantic, Indian, and Pacific oceans.

CHAPTER 13: THE CHOSEN HEIR

A thunderous clap and then a deep hard thud hit the ship. Hanno was back on the ship that was fully engaged in a battle. He sat up in bed and hit the hard top of the bunk bed above him. He stood and felt the cold water rush in. But now the whole bedroom was full of water. And he only felt the cold lower current of water rush in around his tentacles. Hanno and Deyva were out on the stone tablet in the middle of the protected reef. They were both sitting in Lotus position facing each other. Moon was standing nearby watching with concern. Deyva had a bright blue Plava Boya energy coming from her and encircling Hanno. The energy flowed and moved with special shapes, signs, and numbers like an energy formula to help him. Deep inside his head he was that young boy on the ship under attack. This time Deyva was there with him.

"Hanno its ok you are in a safe place. Tell me what you see."

He opened the door and now saw many Luas

fighting against a force of Dacacian warriors. The hull of the lower ship was full of the ocean as a Lua ship would be. Deyva was there with him looking around.

"It's ok keep going."

Hanno saw the sergeant. He was transformed and was swimming with his lower half with eight powerful tentacles. He had a long spear in his hands and was fighting and killing the adversaries all around him.

The man turned to Hanno, "Hanno, you have to get to the balsas!"

Hanno recognizes him, "Its Uncle Hafnia. I had forgotten him. How can I have forgotten him? He trained me and help raise me."

He had a burst of memories of Hafnia and him training in the ocean. Hafnia was teaching him how to fight with the Plava Boya and a Lua spear. Then another memory of them fighting and sparing with Trachanjan short swords. Hanno's Plava Boya was strong as a young child. His energy was moving with his body. He moved the swords so swift and so powerful that he bested his uncle. They shared a laugh as Hanno helped him off the ground. As the memories came back Hanno's own Plava Boya was becoming energized. The energy fields went from Deyva flowing towards him to both their energies growing and encircling them both.

Demetris was with Nerwin making some repairs on his ship. The ship was floating above them.

"Nerwin get me a 3cpo67 socket."

"Right away Captain."

Nerwin waddled as he walked with his heavy tank body. And grabbed the tool from a tool chest nearby.

Demetris looked up and saw Moon, "You know they might be a while. You should check out the cove."

He had perked her interest, "What's the Cove?"

"It's a place the Luas go to relax. Nerwin show Moon the Cove."

"It would be my pleasure Captain."

Nerwin waddled to her, "Want a ride?" He said in a playful voice.

She had been sustained in the reef by either Hanno, Deyva, or Demetris. But with Hanno and Deyva doing a deep dive, Demetris was concerned that she might need more Plava Boya then any of them could provide during the session. Moon jumped into Nerwin's large tank belly and sat in the small seat. It was like riding in a very personal deep sea vessel who could talk to you. Nerwin jumped and then a jet system started propelling him toward the entrance. They passed through the circular stone halls. Instead of going to the right where the Red Lua went to Deyva's study, they went to the left. There were great halls with families of Luas working. Then at the far end of the corridor was a cave that went into the side of what looked like an underground mountain. There was a bright light at the other end of a short walk. Then they came out into the light. And passed through a membrane that held back the sea. Nerwin opened up and Moon stepped out. It was a beach. The entrance had a high rock face that surrounded the membrane entrance. There was beach front and the brightest blue water that looked like an ocean front. It was like being at the beach for humans. Luas were laying out in beach chairs. There were cabanas and other Luas serving drinks. There was some sort of light source high up that resembled the sun. Along the walls, floor, and roof were holes in the sea rocks where other membranes held back the sea on other openings. Moon found herself a beach chair and laid down. Lua children were running and playing. They would run up to the side of a membrane on the wall and jump through it and swim off. Then they would come from somewhere unseen and burst through the roof membrane and drop into the water at the beach. Then get up and run at the other wall and jump through that membrane. It looked like a very fun game to Moon.

Hanno and Deyva had made it up the stairs with Uncle Hafnia. The battle was fully engulfed above deck. But instead of an old human wooden ship as he first remembered it, it was now clearly some advanced Lua ship. There were numerous other battle ships all around them. Several of Blav's dark subs were running alongside Hanno's ship. They were firing on it. Shots of projectiles, energy bolts, and explosions underwater flew all around him. And just like the view of a peaceful ocean to a Lua, the battle sea was also so much more graphic and real. But also all around the ships as they were engulfed in battle was a tumultuous sea. The ships were locked into a huge sea cyclone that stretched far above and far below. The storm was sending bursts of currents in every direction. One of Blav's ships hit the side of the cyclone and was instantly destroyed. As Hanno made it to the side where a rescue ship was attached, he saw Blav. But also something else.

In the stone circle his anger and energy surged and he yelled out, "Father!"

Then to Deyva in the trance, "I remember my father!"

Deyva saw him too, he was below Blav who was fully uncloaked and was this huge black beast. Not Lua but something else. Like a huge dark squid with a man's face and one bright red eye. He was four times the size of Hanno's father. Hanno's father was wearing some sort of dignitary uniform. Both their tentacles were fully engulfed in a battle of grabbing, swiping, and control. Razor sharp hooks on the ends of their tentacles fought and swiped at each other. But also they grabbed and sunk into on another with hook and cup. Blav was winning and overpowering him. Blav had grabbed him about his face and neck with several powerful tentacles but also his powerful arms.

When Blav saw Hanno he arched up and squeezed harder.

Hanno started to rise up off the stone circle. His Plava Boya was surging and overpowering Deyva. She was trying to contain it and help him but it was over taking her.

Then Hanna saw his mother. She was human and his father was extending his Plava Boya over her like Hanno did for Moon. Blav was fighting off ten of the guards who were trying to save Hanno's father while also strangling him. When he squeezed again Hanno could see his father's energy pull away from his mother and saw his mother struggling to breath underwater.

"He's killing them!" Hanno screamed.
Hanno's blue Plava Boya was growing and now coming out of the signs on his chest. When he saw his parents dying his energy changed to bright golden. It filled up the whole bowl of the reef. The burst of energy knocked Deyva back. He had a flood of memories of his parents. Of them playing with him on the beach of an island when he was very young. How his father and him were swimming circles around his mother teasing her. Of a big family table in a large underwater castle. His mother was giving his father a present. Uncle Hafnia was there and many other cousins and friends. It was his father's birthday. As the memories flooded back his energy kept increasing.

Deyva called out, "Demetris help!"
Demetris came out of his ship and they both tried

to use their energies to encircle him but his energy was too powerful.

Then he was back in the battle in the sea. His Uncle Hafnia put Hanno's face in his hand, "Hanno listen to me. You must survive you are the chosen one."

And then there was a huge explosion and Hanno was thrown from the ship. As he drift in the sea unconscious in his memory, his energy slowly came down. In his memory he saw a lone sea turtle playfully beckoning him to swim with him. As Hanno swam he calmed till the bright golden energy absorbed back into his body. He opened his eyes and saw both Deyva and Demetris looking at him.

"I remember everything."

Years Ago, far in the past

Hanno was a young boy. He was moving along some rocks in a dark but beautiful sea mountain. He was swimming and moving over and through cracks and openings in the rocks. Four other Lua boys were moving with him. They were stalking something. Hanno ducked into a large hole and the boys follow. He made a shush sign. A large shadow passed over head. When it passed over the hole, the boys were deep in the dark hole. Several of the boys camouflaged their bodies to match the surrounding rocks. Hanno came out of the hole quickly. His bare upper chest was full of blue markings that extended out of his chest. He had a set of ropes in his hands.

His ten tentacles were out and pushing him as he moved stealthily forward. He made it to the edge of a large rock outcrop. The other boys slowly came up behind him. There was something behind them that moved swiftly. All of the boys this time camouflaged themselves on top of the rocks including Hanno. Their bodies disappeared and matched the colors and texture of the rocks. A huge Lusca beast swam only feet from them. A Lusca was a beast that was shark in the front and squid in the back. Its tentacles were long and powerful.

Hanno took off and appeared to jump but also swim off the cliff edge, "Cowabunga!"
His rope landed perfectly over the nose and head of the Lusca. And Hanno landed on its back above its fin. The beast exploded with anger. It tried to turn on itself and grab him with its large shark mouth. But Hanno held on. The other boys were yelling and following at a distance.

"Go Hanno, you are the king of the sea."
The beast then used several of its tentacles to try and grab him from behind. But he was too high up and just bent over near the back of the beast. His tentacles were wrapped tightly around the beast and his hooks were sunk in to its flesh.

"Woo, woo, Hanno isn't afraid of anything."
The beast then tried to swim fast and flip him off making wild moves up, down, side to side. As the beast made its way wildly away from the rocks it headed through a very large seam in a huge sea

mountain. On the other side of the seam was the Capital of Kerajaan a city called Alaeze. The city was built along the sea floor but also grew up the sides of the Sea Mountains. From high up at the top of the mountain, from the eyes of a Lua it looked like the most beautiful protected valley. And from a human's eyes this would be completely invisible; but there even was a water fall that came up over the far side of the valley. It was a water current that was denser and colder and thus moved, fell, and then pooled at the base of the valley. To Luas it was a truly aesthetic addition to the valley. The houses built into the walls were made of stone, marble, and other precious metals. The shapes and structures better resembled cathedrals and castles.

The Lusca burst into the valley and everyone noticed it like a bull that was let loose on a small village. It busted through several street vendors and knocked out the wall of a home. Hanno still held on. Then it swam up right in the middle for everyone to see. The other boys arrived and saw what a great problem this was turning out to be. The Lusca then changed rapidly again and tried to swim with his top toward the mountain. Hanno adjust and expanded his Plava Boya and a blue force field formed. So as the beast busted into the side of cliff house and then swam along the cliff walls Hanno was protected and still holding on. The noise and commotion was so great that everyone in the city stopped and watched. Uncle

Hafnia now dressed in full warrior guard could be seen working in the court as a Kings guard. Hafnia, and Hanno's Mother and father came out on a balcony to see what was going on. In the center of town was a tall tower that had on it a special clock. With each move and crack the Lusca gave Hanno, his power was weakening. The Lusca swam at the clock.

Hafnia saw it, "On me!"
Hafnia and a squad of warriors moved on the position. The beast busted right through the middle of the clock tower. Hanno fell off and was knocked unconscious. He floated in the sea. The beast turned and then swam right at him with mouth open and razor sharp teeth prepared to strike. Hafnia threw a sharp long sea spear and it moved through the water as it spun. It was clearly designed to be thrown in this manner. It spiked into the Lusca through its hardened head and deep into its skull. Although it had been killed, its momentum caused it to eerily drift right up and close to Hanno. Hanno came to, looking right into the huge toothy mouth of the dead Lusca.

Later Hanno had cleaned up and changed. He was walking on his feet and legs in a lonely dark hall. It was a back entrance to the court of His father. A large delegate of creatures that looked like Blav were talking with Hanno's mother and father.

Blav opened his squid folds revealing his one red eye, "Honorable King Hanno Kekoa, first of his name. Your Luas have ruled Kerajaan for ten generations. The Mahracs must seed. We have been ushered into our small sea left to die."

Hanno the first answered him, "By the Nevige Treaty you were given the Bakland Sea."

Hanno's mother, Madam Genvi added, "Baron Blav your house was the first to sign the treaty and now only five years after the war, you want more sea?"

Blav looked at his companions and then back at the king and queen. He lifted up off the floor slightly and opened his hood even wider. His red eye was captivating and hypnotic. Hafnia stepped forward holding his battle spear. He had on sea armor that covered his chest, shoulders, and back. He also had matching bracers on his forearms. On his back were two Trachanjan swords. Hanno was behind the throne eavesdropping. King Kekoa waived off Hafnia.

Blav continued, "When my house signed the treaty we signed it with the understanding that we would be allowed to live. And for Mahracs to live, we must spawn."

Hanno could hear Hafnia when he said under his breath, "Spawn, more like poison the sea."

The King answered, "You can spawn in the Bakland Sea as the treaty states."

Blav became heated, "You know this means death to all living Mahracs."

Genvi just said, "From death comes life."

Blav closed his face flap and left. His eye glowed so bright red could be seen coming out of his seam. When he passed Hafnia and also young Hanno hiding in the hall. Hanno camouflaged himself into the wall.

And then he heard Blav say, "We will see what life will come from your deaths my King and Queen."

Hanno woke from a soft sleep in the study of Deyva wondering on his past.

Moon had found her spot on a lounge chair at the Cove. She had on sunshades and was sipping a strawberry looking ice drink. Slowly and suddenly her shades were lifted by one tentacle, her drink was stolen by another and a third softly covered her eyes.

"Guess who?"

She sat up, "Hanno?"

He was sitting on a lounge chair next to her drinking her drink and wearing her shades. As he removed his tentacle so she could see, he retracted them and transformed to his legs in front of her. He was wearing a swimming suit. She noticed that transformation and saw it up close for the first time.

"How far up do they...erh...um...I mean..go..?"

She was motioning toward his legs in the shorts.

"Let's just say the parts you may or may not be talking about are very human, so don't you worry."

"Maybe you'll show me some day?"

Hanno found himself more embarrassed than she was, but they both blushed.

"Come on."

He grabbed her hand and they playfully jogged toward the side wall. He then dove through the membrane and she stopped in the sand. A tentacle came back and grabbed her and pulled her through the membrane. Hanno and Moon can be seen swimming and playing in the water outside the cove. Moon then came out of the roof membrane and dropped twenty feet doing a flip and a half and then dove into the ocean floor. Hanno followed after her as if they were playing chase. Several Lua children joined in on the fun. Moon swam in the ocean so fast she was using her feet and legs like a mermaid. Then jumped out of the ocean and flew through the air and dove into the other side membrane and was off in the water again. Several children were running and then swimming after her. Hanno was playfully chasing all of them, moving and grabbing youngens. He used of all of the tentacles as he grab, swam, and threw a kid out of a membrane, while still chasing her. They were in the ocean outside but near the roof membrane. She tried to go past him on the left while all the remaining youngsters went to the right. He grabbed three little ones in a tentacle each and then grabbed her with two around her legs and torso. Then the whole pack busted through the roof membrane and splashed down near and old couple of Luas floating near the beach. The whole group busted into laughter. The kids ran and swam off. Hanno and Moon embraced with a slow sweet hug with their arms above water. And then also were entwined with her legs, feet, and his tentacles below water. This was the closest their bodies had been. They kissed a soft passionate kiss. And the whole beach noticed the young love.

CHAPTER 14: THE ASSEMBLY OF THE AMERICAS

Lord Cadel was working in a small captains quarters. He was at his desk air typing with his hands a letter that was populating straight to a virtual screen. The walls of the quarters behind him were translucent and show the outside of The Order's Command flying battleship. It showed a beautiful bright view that overlooked flooded lands. The lands below were full of all sorts of jungle plants and trees. The ship started to change altitude going up and the fauna changed too. Here the lands were dryer filled with more deciduous forests.

"Commander we are ten minutes out."

Speaking into his PDS, "Copy that."

He swiped his hand and the translucent walls turn off and are now hardened thick walls outlining the small quarters. Leaving out he passed several crew mates. They were dressed in battle security uniforms. He was carrying a cup of coffee delicately balancing it as he passed crew mates in the narrow corridors.

"Commander."

One passed and saluted in respect. At a junction point the corridor passes through to an open area. To both the right and the left gunners sat in rotating gunner chairs. The chairs had virtual screens all around the airmen. As the operators swept the area, guns below and above moved. The design created a three hundred and sixty degree shooting platform on both sides. He continued forward and arrived at the bridge of the ship. As the ship flew over the region, the ship was twice the size of a stealth bomber and three times in height. There were no windows visible, but from within the bridge a full translucent view in every direction was visible. Off in the distance were rising hills leading up to a mountain top where no trees grew. Atop the highest mountain was Backbone station. A tall Watchtower atop the mountain stuck up high over the whole region. Inside the tower operators were watching The Order's ship approach on a very sophisticated command and control system. The operators in the tower were more rugged than you would expect.

The primary Operator speaking into a prewar radio system, "Tower to base come in."

"Base go ahead."

"New Atlanta is arriving."

"Copy that."

"Tower to forward posts"

Several military squads in full green camo were positioned at artillery stations at four different points within a mile radius of the tower.

"Post command go ahead."

"Dignitaries arriving, stand down."

"Copy that all Forward Posts copy?"

All responded. As the ship passed over the area, multiple artillery posts watched with caution and even tracked their guns with their passing. Within The Order's ship control screen a much more high-tech system identified and target locked on all cannon positions. But no order to fire was given.

A view over the region looking down on the earth, off in the distance to the South was New Atlanta much smaller from this far away. And to the Northwest the huge floating city over the great lakes known as Laurentian. Backbone Mountain was about half way between the two great future cities. The station sat atop of the Allegheny Mountains near the Continental Divide. And was one of the more prosperous ground settlements. They somehow survived the war being far enough away from population centers and nuclear strikes. And then later high enough to avoid the flooding. As Lord Cadel unloaded with his entourage including Detective Denton and several other commanders. The Laurentian ships were also arriving to the other side of the air strip. Already landed were three of the Blav's dark subs. The Laurentian ambassador and his associates wore light sleek jump suits. They looked like they had been on a space adventure from the sixties. So different from the retro London styled suits of the Atlantians. The two leaders stepped aside for a greeting.

"Lord Cadel it's been too long."

Cadel shook hands, "Ambassador Lykaios so good to see you. What has it been, since the nationals?"

"Yes and I seemed to remember your son going home with three gold medals."

"You're too kind."

Lykaios leaning in, "So sorry to hear about your daughter."

The gesture was disguised as a concern, but was clearly meant as a put down.

"Well you know what they say, The Order will lead the lost home."

"Very well put. Let me ask you Jason."

Few felt privilege to address Cadel so commonly.

"Why have we agreed to meet with the unworthy?"

"Well honestly I know they cannot be trusted but having an alliance with them may help with our other problem. But I actual do need their help locating my daughter."

The two city delegates entered into the tower. It was built with all natural wood and had glass all around. There was a large hall that was set with tables. The room had a floor to ceiling glass wall facing the forest and surrounding area. Out the windows to the east was a waterfall that ran down into a river that then passed right in front of the outer deck of the center. Outside several camouflaged soldiers patrolled with old world rifles. Along the back walls were elevated seats for the staff. At one end of the table was Baron Blav. He appeared in the most human form that we have ever seen him. Although he still had on a dark cloak and hood. But within the hood an actual face appeared. His skin was grey and dark and had some sort of light smoke on the edges. He sat with several of his commanders.

Down at the entrance of the coral reef bowl Nerwin and Demetris were at the front of the Cheonia. They had a panel lowered revealing internal controls and engine operations. They were upgrading and repairing the ship. Deyva and Tellua were pushing a floating cart up under the back of the ship.

Deyva to Demetris, "D ready for lift."

"Sure thing beautiful."

Tellua shared a look with Deyva as Demetris moved his energy. The Cheonia dive chamber opened and then the energy from the ship lifted the cart up into it.

Tellua asked "Deyva what is going on there?"

They were walking back inside to get more supplies.

"Well it's been the long game. We can never seem to stay in one place long enough for romance.

He is always on some mission. And now with this latest mission."

Deyva nodded toward Hanno. They kept walking and talking as we now were moving with Moon and Hanno toward the ship. They were packing up also. Moon and Hanno passed them and now too were below the chamber. Demetris saw them and opened the chamber door. They then swam up into the ship. The ships Plava Boya was also pressurizing the chamber holding back the sea. Moon and Hanno passed through the field.

"Hanno what have you learned about the Plava Boya?"

"Well Deyva says it is the 'Imperium Amara', or Power of God."

They were putting their supplies into the sleeping pod that she had been using.

"Power of God that is so interesting. The bible talks about the power of God filling believers as well, but you never hear of it being able to be seen."

"Well the Luas stories tell that God gave them the power. And they learned how to harness it and store it and regenerate it like a fuel source."

"I overheard Demetris and Deyva talking that you had a different type of Boya. Something they had never seen called the 'Aureum Imperium. Are you like some sort of prophet?"

"I don't feel like a prophet. I'm just a guy who a few months ago was meeting a nice girl in my science class."

He grabbed her and leaned in for a kiss, which was quickly interrupted. As everyone boarded the ship.

Including Nerwin who waddled between them, "Ah young love is as deep as the ocean and wet as the sea."

This time both Moon and Hanno were blushing. Deyva smiled also a little but then she changed and looked at Demetris for explanation.

"What I got him from an old scrapper ship." Demetris and Deyva took the two front seats and Demetris closed the doors and started to power up the ship. His hands floated over the controls and his blue Plava Boya reached out and took control of screens, switches and dials and then the engines that fired up with full power. Moon and Hanno sat in the back two chairs.

"Where to?" Moon asked

Demetris pulled up a map of the oceans floors, "Chathair."

Demetris adjusted his navigational system and locked in the target.

Hanno this time spoke up, "Chathair I thought we were going to La Venta?"

"No one even approaches the Gulf Of Mexico, the Bahamas, or even South America especially from the sea without first getting a visa from the Dacacian city of Chathair."

Moon worried, "Dacacians isn't that the green lizard fish creatures trying to kill Hanno?"

The ship started pulling out of the reef. Many

of Deyva's friends were outside the entrance and were waving but also some of them were swimming to follow them off.

"Blav only hires Dacacian Militia. The Dacacians are sentient creatures that lived with us on Syrena. There were many races of sea folk on Syrena. We were actually on a mission of transporting a contingent of Dacacian immigrants to a newly formed seabed when we hit the strange storm. Syrena was rich with life. But like many of God's creatures, the Dacacians have chosen good and bad paths. Chathair is their...how do you say... Capital within your world."

Moon fascinated, "Like the bartender?"

"Right like our bartender."

Hanno smiling, "You went to a Bar?"

"Oh yes it was amazing and scary."

Moon fixed a sly grin, "Nerwin do you know how to make a Sunrise-Down?"

Nerwin started moving toward the galley, "Right away Miss Moon."

Moon just looked at Hanno, "You're going to love this."

All had sat at the table. The table was full of delegates from several communities including the two floating cities. There was the delegates of the Desert Front. A large underground city on the edge of the deserted wilderness somewhere just west of what used to be the Rockies. Then there was the ground city of the massive dome called Four Corners. It resided on the corners of the former Kansas, Missouri, Oklahoma, and Arkansas borders. And then several other regional leaders like Backbone station that were smaller. Many of whom left weeks earlier to arrive at the station for the meet up via horseback, jeep, and old world planes.

The leader of Backbone station, Col. Davies was a man in his early seventies. He had fought in the war to secure the region and was foundational at setting up this settlement. The settlement and the surrounding region had become famous for grounder cooperation. Even the floating cities were envious at his diplomatic abilities and came to him to help negotiate their disagreements. During the war he was a commander of an elite group of fighters and was feared and respected as a leader. No one was confused by his current humble appearance with a full white beard, white pony tail and balding forehead. He wore clothes that appeared made out of old military surplus camos, deer hides, ropes, and if possible tree leaves.

Davies opened, "Thank you for everyone here who has agreed to this meeting. We at Backbone station do appreciate all of your trade and many of you brought gifts of resources for our community. So regardless of what is decided here, we thank you. The floor is open to Lord Cadel who requested this meeting."

Cadel stood, "There are two proposals to the assembly. One to allow Blav and the Mahrac fleet and their sentiments access to the primary signal. And two, to allow Baron Blavalotski a seat at the assembly."

He paused to let the proposal set in, "Many of you here know that I have a grave personal agenda involved in this request. The loss of my daughter at the hands of the sea folk kidnapping, may lead you to believe that I have not considered the full depth of this request. I must admit I am blinded with rage at my own personal loss. But let me remind you that I had made this same proposal twenty two years ago when the Eurasia three shut themselves off from the rest of the world. Which in turn has led to our current cold war."

Cadel was referring to the three floating cities that hovered over the Mediterranean, Arabian Gulf, and the Yellow Sea and their alignment against the North American cities.

"So in full knowledge of my personal agenda, I want you to realize the great benefit this alliance could be in our current international conflict. Thank you."

Lord Cadel sat down and before his butt hit the seat, Ambassador Lykaios from Laurentian stood to speak, "Thank you Lord Cadel for bringing this to the assembly. As the Order pronounces 'May logic and education help you see you through this great difficulty'. And to you Baron Blav so nice to see you at the table."

When Lykaios spoke, every word was full of arrogance and an air of looking down on everyone at the table. He was a thin man in his late fifties with dark black hair and a white swish across the front. His sleek suit appeared to come straight out of a sixties space science fiction magazine. The shininess of his suit and the clean pale appearance of his protected city skin made him stand out. Most of the regents at the table were dark and earthy in appearance.

"During the last siege before the airships were put into the trade association many of you remember what it was like to be land locked by the current formidable seas. Constant storms and impassable currents kept us isolated from the rest of the world. The sea folk were the only ones who could navigate deep under the oceans threats. During that time, did the Mahracs come to our aid? Did the Luas come to our aid? No not one."

Blav's smoke from within his hood. Smoke could be seen to be streaming and building and spilling out in dark hatred. But he held his tongue.

"The launch of our cargo airships and the primary signal led us back from the brink. It is our pure encrypted communications. If this fell into the hands of the enemy…"

Blav couldn't take it any further he stormed out of his seat, "Are you calling us your enemy? We come to you and offer our help."

Lykaios was still standing, Cadel stood too.

Then when Davies stood the room took notice, "Gentlemen one speaker at a time. Lykaios do you yield to the Baron?"

Lykaios arrogantly responded, "No I do not yield."

Blav spoke over him anyways, "We have lived in the shadows for long enough. Our numbers have risen and we are many. We will not be treated like second class citizens. Soon we may just rise up out of the sea and take the land too."
Lykaios looked around to see if everyone heard what he heard. Cadel had too much at stake.

Lykaios attacked back, "If that was meant as a threat you can guarantee it will be met with force."

Davies putting his hands up and motioning for everyone to sit down, "Men please."

Cadel took a moment in a brooding pause, "Ambassador Lykaios did you not recently tell me that your broken trade association with Bakinh was deeply hurting your food stocks?"
The republic of Bakinh was a grouping of floating vessels rather than a floating city. It floated over the Celebes Sea that was comprised of the survivors of Thailand, Malaysia, Philippines, and Indonesia.
Lykaios face softened.

"Blav although you have been successful in the sea, didn't you mention that your sentiments lack metallurgic resources? This alliance could bring the land and the sea together. By giving Blav access to the primary signal we extend our intelligence network and can gain an edge against the Eastern Alliance."

Lykaios spoke up, "And help you locate your daughter."

He meant it to point out the self-serving goals of Cadel but Cadel took ownership.

"Your right and they could help me find my daughter. Sorry but do you not have a family of your own. Would you not do anything you could?" During the whole speech Denton sat at the back wall. He was there to support Cadel. He was there as the lead investigator trying to locate Moon for Cadel. Anything he had to say to the assembly should have been filtered through all of Cadel's advisors and then Cadel himself. But Denton wasn't a man who cared about protocol.

Denton stood and approached the table, "Yes giving Blav and his thugs access to our communication network would most definitely help locate Moon. And I do want to try and find your daughter. But at what cost? I was first infantry during the sea siege when the Mahracs fought to take Charleston. If it weren't for New Atlanta and the enormous military advantage a weaponized floating city gave us, we would have lost that war. And Blav and his forces were there fighting side by side with the Luas and the Dacacians. It was this assembly and its forces that blew them back into the sea. And now we are allowing them to join the assembly?"

Davies again tried to bring the meeting to order. This time there was cross arguing and yelling from all sides, "Gentlemen, Gentlemen,

Damn it, shut up!"

The room got quiet. All knew that the Col. had fought boots on the ground in many wars including the sea siege. When all of them hid behind their delegates and protections forces, he led the fight.

He then continued as if nothing upset him, "Anyone else?"

No one else had anything to say.

"Then it's up for a vote. Those for letting the Mahracs in, raise your hand."

A slow sweep of the voting members of the assembly showed a majority and sided with Cadel.

CHAPTER 15: THE SIGSBEE ABYSSAL PLAIN

The Cheonia sliced through the ocean like a space ship in the heavens. The sun was just starting to rise far above but with their Lua eyes the beams cut through the ocean and lit up the underwater world. The ship was coming up from deep below the surface. Deyva was alone in the pilot's seat. She had her tentacles out and they spread out all over both seats and all over the controls. But it wasn't ugly like a large squid. It was soft and beautiful like many long legs. She was wearing a sort of t-shirt and shorts and her form was noticeable. Her tentacles only added to her loveliness. Her hands were holding a cup of tea in front of her. One tentacle was thumbing through a virtual screen. Another she was swishing softly below her chair, like a cat swishing its tail. And still another was propped up against the back of the seat. The surrounding 360 view of the bridge was similar to that of a plane flying up the side of a steep mountain. With one exception, the mountain was deep underwater. Back in the galley, Nerwin was locked and charging in his charging station when he sensed movement. It was Moon coming out of her Pod into the galley. She was wearing a t-shirt and panties carrying a blanket.

When one of Nerwin's eyes opened on his face screen she put a finger to her mouth, "Shshsh."

She tiptoed and then slowly opened Hanno's Pod. He was sound asleep. The inside of the ship was kept dry in case one of the Luas during sleep somehow unconsciously pulled back their Boya that protected and provided for Moon's underwater survival. When she entered Hanno's room, he had the all the wall screens visibly open to the ocean. It was like stepping into an aquarium. He was laying on his back with his chest and stomach exposed. A blanket covered his mid-section and then his tentacles were out and everywhere. They were dark blue with black tiger stripes throughout. One was stretched out of the bed and on the floor. She slowly stepped closer and touched it with her hand. And as if the tentacle itself responded to her touch it turned to the color of human skin and softened. Then began to shrink back up under the covers. She lifted the covers and crawled in to snuggle. As her legs and arms moved to get closer to him, his body responded and he softly moved and surrounded her with his. They lay there sweetly as he slowly woke up.

"Where'd you come from?"

She smiled, "Oh who me? I've been here all night."

And they shared a smile they then shared a kiss. Suddenly through the view of his room a whole pod of dolphins swam and encircled the vessel. They were jumping and swimming all around them. We follow the dolphins and can see them from the bridge view too. The view from the bridge showed the Cheonia was at the top of the ridge and was now passing through the bright blue shallow seas of the Bahamas. The dolphins followed them playfully. Soon Demetris, Moon, and Hanno all joined Deyva at the bridge.

Moon asked, "Where are we?"

Deyva looking at her charts, "Just passed the Lesser Antilles into the Caribbean Sea."

Demetris took over the controls and Deyva stretched from her night duties.

"Not much farther now."

It was all new and exciting for both Moon and Hanno. But Deyva and Demetris were cautious and aware of potential dangers ahead.

Moon interjected, "In my great, great, great grandma's on-line travel journal I found in the archives, she mentioned going on a great floating hotel that floated on the sea around the Caribbean. She even had pictures."

Demetris countered, "Well this isn't the Caribbean your grandma knew."

In front of them in the Venezuelan Basin was the city of Chathair. From above the ocean surface towers, platforms, and buildings could be seen as beige and red earth like shapes. From the sky it might appear as some natural phenomena of eroded rocks and pillars coming out of the sea. But below the surface of the water the shapes reveal a massive city with fortified walls and gates surrounding the whole city. The shallow waters of the Caribbean looked down on the entrance of the city.

"Blvark tuk mehreck fron."

Far behind them past the blue sea in the dark ocean a Mahrac sub lurked. The sub commander not too different but slightly smaller than Blav communicated on the water channel.

Blav responded back, "Mehreck fron twej."

Blav from somewhere deep in the ocean logged in his charts the location of the Cheonia. As the Cheonia was pulling into an elevated landing pad below the sea but outside the city gates; the Mahrac scout ship had closed the gap and was now in the Caribbean.

Then to the Mahrac communications officer a call came in, "NH 122 niner to MR 99 we saw your ping request go ahead with your transmissions."

The communications officer to his commander, "Verjk dwgwick."

Then to the New Atlantean vessel, "Copy that NH 122 niner. Sending you the location of the scum kidnappers now."

Rising up out of the ocean over the Mahrac sub, the structures of Chathair were visible. The Dacacians, like amphibian creatures, live in both the sea and the land. Dacacians although from a sea planet, quickly and better adapted to the earth. From high above, the impact of the melting polar ice caps were clearer. In the Southwestern US, North America's higher elevations pushed back the sea and most of the land was dry. But in the former state of Mexico, the Eastern mountain chain known as the Sierra Madre Oriental had been destroyed by a nuclear attack on Mexico City. So the water from the Gulf had filled in and flooded most of the country. This same flooding had wiped out Central America, the Caribbean Islands, California and Florida; all disappeared. To the south, South America still rose up out of the sea. So between North and South America, now the Atlantic and the Pacific oceans met between the two great continents.

The small crew made their way off the ship. Hanno's Boya covered Moon. The platform was old and ancient. So too was the gate and the wall. The platform looked down on the gate.

"Where is everyone?" Moon asked.

Deyva just looked at her. The look she gave her, quieted the young girl.

They walked to the edge of the platform and then Demetris jumped and started to swim down to the gate entrance. They were all in their battle gear which made it easier for the Luas to switch back and forth from their human form to their Lua one. Their armor was more similar to that of ancient Greek warriors of old with Cuirass armor that was shaped to the muscles of the upper body but left lots of free movement below the loins. The wide opening also allowed free deployment of tentacles. They swam down and Moon swam more like a dolphin with a flipper kick. She was shoeless and she used newly webbed, elongated feet. They made it to the bottom of the wall. The wall and the fortified gate stretched from the sea bed up and came out of the sea several hundred feet. The top of the wall was capped with a mixture of manmade and sea made sharp rock and corral. With the exception of an airship, through the gate was the only way in. They made it to the landing and immediately the signs of battle were everywhere. One section of the wall was blasted and broken. The guard towers were riddled with sea spears and explosive damage. Then they arrived at the gate and Demetris pulled his massive gun from his back. All froze. Then Moon saw it. The massive gates were broken and hanging strangely in place. Deyva looked out into the sea behind them looking for threats. As if she could sense the Mahracs just out of sight. Demetris slowly looked into the opening. Then he entered. The place was desolate. The great city that once was the center of all Dacacians life was now a city of ruins. They all slowly moved through the open gates. Inside there were walls and buildings in every direction. All vacant of life.

Deyva observed, "Look corral has started to form on the gates. This didn't just happen. When was the last time you were here D?"

"It has been several years maybe a little longer."

Moon passed a shop that had toys for baby Dacacians. There were small Dacacian warrior replicas. And her heart sunk thinking of the children.

Moon offered, "Maybe they had to move."

Then Hanno stopped and floated up slightly, "Not all of them."

The others floated up to him. Up on the secondary walls that protected the inner city were the bones and bodies of killed Dacacian warriors. The one near Hanno was full of large thick arrows. They made their way up the main street. It went to the right and then started up a hill toward the city center. Demetris and Deyva were on point. Hanno and Moon behind all looking both right and left. There were so many empty buildings, many broken and falling down from some sort of artillery fire. Others empty with their doors open from some mass evacuation. Demetris had his gun out and he was holding it tactically with both hands clearing piles and debris looking for what might lurk behind. Deyva had a staff that was made with holes through out, designed to move tactically through water. Although the city was still bright and full of colors, Moon even seeing through the Lua eyes, the lifelessness made it seem darker. In the darkness she saw a small pink flower. As Moon moved toward the flower, Hanno also saw something in the other direction. He pulled his knives out as he looked into an opening. The building Hanno entered appeared to be some sort of military structure within the city. Maybe a guard house or a police station. In the front entrance, some great battle had been fought.

"Demetris you have to see this."
Both Demetris and Deyva made their way to him. There was bodies everywhere. Mostly Dacacians but then they saw it. A large Mahrac. He had a large projectile weapon and had dropped twenty or so Dacacians before going down himself.

"I think we know who attacked the city." Demetris said plainly.

Deyva added, "Mahracs"
Then it was as if Hanno felt Moon had disconnected or rather been cut off from his Boya. He looked behind him and realized Moon had not come in with the others. He moved out onto the street and didn't see her there either.

"Moon! Moon where are you?"
The vibrations in his calls moved through the water throughout the city.

Just before Hanno had found the military building, we go back and see Moon approaching the flower. She reached down to grab it and it moved and floated away in the water. She smiled and looked back at Hanno but then went after it.

The flower was floating on a small current. She followed playfully even having to swim to catch up to it. The flower led her to a higher balcony. The balcony led to a gazebo inside a mansion built. She swam into to the gazebo and landed on a cold marble floor. The flower slowly moved along the ground just inside a large glass covered room. Moon walked toward it and reached down to grab it. Suddenly she was transported back home. She was in her open atrium looking out over New Atlanta. The air was clear and the sky was beautiful blue. She breathed in a huge breath and then exceled.

"Don't you have homework to do my little sweet one?"

She turned and saw her mom, "Momma."

It's like she was in a dream. She ran to her mother.

"I've missed you."

She gave her the biggest hug. Her mother hugged her back and kissed her on her head.

"You better hurry, I think I hear your father."

Just then the door opened and her father and brother came in.

"Well you need to keep training. Seven days a week if you want to go to Nationals."

Her father was happy and she was so glad to see all of them. She was in shock. They all gathered at the table on the balcony as food was served by small service drones. They were all engaged in conversation and full of joy and laughter. She just watched them in the sun and air on the balcony. She had forgotten about the good times.

Hanno nervously searched from building to building shouting out for Moon. Demetris caught him as he moved from one to the other.

"Hanno calm down, we will find her."
He had to grab him by the shoulders. With his blood up, Hanno brought up several tentacles and grabbed both of Demetris hands and pulled them off of him.

Deyva stopped them, "Boys can we work as a team."
Deyva was near the center court yard outside the military building.

"I'll stay here maybe she will find her way back. The two of you work together and do a logical grid search of the area. And push out your Boya you may sense her before you see her."

Both men turn their stern looks to soften and say in unison, "Makes sense."
Building by building they moved as a team. They had searched the mansion on the first floor but in the darkness missed the door to the second floor. They moved on. There was a set of mansions that lined that particular wall. On the next one down they did find a stairwell. Demetris was searching an upper study. The lobby had several columns but not stairs. A common sea folk design that went up three stories. Demetris was slowly floating up and searching. Hanno was on the second floor that led out to a balcony. Both mansion balconies had been

damaged by the battle. There were huge chunks of floor and wall missing. Then Hanno saw it. It reflected in the sea light. A Trachanjan sword. Hanno went after it and it too floated on a current slowly away from him. He then fully released his tentacles and swam after it. The faster he swam the faster it floated away. He found himself on the same balcony at the same dark entrance where Moon had gone.

Far off across the city a lone warrior came out of the shadows. He was tall, long, and full of muscles. He was deep sea green in color. He was up on a high tower along the opposite wall. From a small hidden place he moved forward. He was wearing a dark brown hood over his head. He lifted a strong long sea bow with two left hands and then with his two right hands positioned two massive arrows within a set of bow strings. He stretched out his front leg straight sitting on a bent back leg. Then he pulled the huge bow strong with his two right hands. The two arrows appeared to be made of bone and hardened sea rock mined from deep in the ocean. The arrows were dark and had long sharp jagged points with razor sharp tips. He held and his muscles flexed.

Hanno bent down and as his hand was only inches away from the sword, the warrior released the arrows. Both arrows flew through the sea as if the design of the bow released them into a spinning pattern. They spun around an unseen center forcefully heading right at Hanno. But before Hanno could grab the sword it turned into a long dark vine right in front of him. He heard a loud noise and looked up into the darkness. Demetris was at his side within seconds. In the room the two arrows plunged into a two story high jelly fish. But none like anything Hanno had ever seen. The soft floating hood was dying from the impact of the arrows. They followed the beasts tentacles down to attached pods. In the pods were creatures. Some were only bones but in others were dead Dacacians. Then they saw her. It was Moon captured inside one of the pods. They made their way quickly to her.

"I wouldn't do that if I were you." The warrior was now right behind them.
They were still in shock and frozen for fear of harming Moon. She was floating in the pod with her eyes open. She was not looking at them, but into the fantasy world the jelly had created.

"You have to cut the radial canal and separate it from the exumbrella before you can remove her."
He pulled a large knife. He made short work of the beast cutting and separating it.

"If you would have touched it, you would have been put her into shock. It has an electrified exterior shell."

Hanno asked, "What is it?"

The mysterious Dacacian answered, "You've heard of Lion's Mane Jelly. Well this is its big brother."

Then the man carefully cut Moon from the pod and as she slipped out as Hanno caught her.

"I am Grim Jeshile, thirteenth of his name." And as a Dacacian custom he reached out both his massive right hands to shake. Demetris and Hanno strangely each shook one. Hanno carried and floated Moon. They all then made their way out the terrace and down to Deyva below. Deyva quickly moved into her medic mode and took some medicine from a pack. Hanno was at Moon's side holding her hand.

Demetris to Grim, "What happened here?"

"Well I've actually been migrating from south to north for my Mutba."

Demetris knew about the Dacacians Mutba. It was their custom to migrate great distances before choosing a mate and procreating.

"I'm from Chontales just south of the Cordillera pass. I was heading to Chathair for a little sun and fun."

His lizard like face smiled a smile all men identify with. When Grim spoke, he stood head and shoulder taller than Demetris. He stretched and flexed his massive arms. Dacacians had adapted into tight culture classes. Grim was clearly from the warrior class. But it was unusual to find a lone warrior not affiliated with a unit, division, or battle group. Demetris had traveled and traded with Dacacians for several centuries. And had even been to cities to the south. Chontales was a smaller city along a sea mountain where the former country of Nicaragua once resided.

Chathair was not only the center of politics, industry and trade for the Dacacians but it also was a place of leisure, pleasure, and yes mating. To the North of the city was the Plyacades, an above water section of the city that had massive pools, waterfalls, and streams that flowed through the city and down into the ocean. And plenty of sunning and mating areas.

Grim continued, "I arrived a week ago and could not believe what I saw."

Demetris challenged him, "You didn't hear about it on the Semptac?"

Semptac was a communication network used by Dacacians. Luas communicated with their Boya but sometimes used the Semptac when dealing with Dacacians. Malracs had their own network, but their spies knew of it and were suspected of hacking it.

"No not a word."

"To what Iqela are you attached?"

"No Iqela, just me."

"That's not very common, is it?"

"Grim is unique."

Moon started coming out of her trance. She initially was covered in the Jelly's goo. Hanno and Deyva had cleaned her off. She was back to normal. She started to stand.

"What happened?"

Hanno answered, "You were caught in a giant Jelly fish."

She smiled at him like he was joking, "No really?"

They helped her walk seeing how she felt. Then she saw Grim. He was not like the bartender who was smaller and a part of the servant class. She hid behind Hanno.

"It's ok, this is the one who saved you."

Grim almost bowed seeing she was human and that of an upper class human.

"My lady it was my honor. I am Grim Jeshile, thirteenth of his name."

This time he only presented to her his lower hand. When she shook it, he held her gently. She smiled sweetly from receiving his respect and attention. Then at the same moment both Grim and Demetris felt the movement in the seas and turned their heads toward the broken gate. The sea folk like so many other sea creatures could sense danger from very far distances. All looked toward the gate and there was a dark periscoping as if they saw through the broken gate, behind the blue Bahamian waters and into the deep dark sea. And the dark looked back.

Demetris then said to the group, "We have to move."

Grim instinctually, "Come on."

CHAPTER 16: THOUGHTS OF HOME

Grim led the pack swimming using all four arms in a breast stroke while also moving his torso and side to side. If it weren't for the Plava Boya, the Luas and Moon would never been able to keep up. They swam up the main street into the political square. The structures farther into the city had less damage. The materials used were clearly some combination of resources available on earth but with mastery gained from underwater living on Syrena. The material looked like marble but had earth tones. It was smooth with intricate designs and carvings. They followed Grim to the North and then almost instinctually when they arrived at the massive staircase to Plyacades they floated down and began to walk. They were exhausted. Moon was breathing water through the Boya. She felt like she did when she used to run. The stair case was as wide as a city block at the base. It was lined with wonderfully designed pillars.

And it narrowed at the top. All were catching their breaths while constantly looking back. But nothing followed them.

Deyva spoke first, "What was that?"

Demetris answered, "I know I felt it too. I've never felt anything like that before."

Hanno asked, "I felt it too. Like…"

"Like being swallowed by the darkness." Grim said calmly surprising the others.

He approached the top of the staircase and looked back one more time. He stepped out of the sea and into the Plyacades.

He added, "I thought I would be molting and taking in the sun and other" looking at young Moon adjusted what he was going to say, "and enjoying cool drinks. Not running from a Giant Cthulhu."

Deyva stopped half in the water and half out, "Excuse me."

Moon actually knew this one from a book she read, "Oh I know this one. A Cthulhu is a beast from H.P. Lovecraft novel with a squidy face and dragon like body and wings. I read it on the PDS interweb. But I thought it was a mythical creature."

Demetris met Grim on the top of the landing and the others followed, "Ah maybe on earth but not on Syrena."

Then to Grim, "And let me add an extinct creature on Syrena."

Grim kind of brush off or rather didn't notice

Demetris and Deyva's concern.

"Datos are not extinct."

Grim walked through an entrance garden where native Dacacian species of fruit trees grew. He grabbed two large melons with his two left hands and took turns feeding his face alternating hands as he fed.

Demetris hoping his new acquaintance was misunderstanding something, "Datos are six feet in length and are docile. There hasn't been a Giant Cthulhu on Syrena for a millennia. And none not even a Datos ever spotted on earth."

Grim past a field that lay open before the pools. He stopped and looked out as if he was fantasying on might have been.

"Don't tell that to Jimbo."

Deyva said it out loud but the whole group mouth it in disbelief, "Jimbo!?!"

"Yeah he spends most his time down at what the humans call, point Nemo. But lately he has been feeding more and more to the North."

They looked at him in disbelief but then started adjusting packs and supplies.

"Let's rest here for the night."

Grim grabbed five lounge beds with his four hands and drug them to the group.

"Might as well be in comfort."

Grim started a fire and was roasting a Capybara and flavoring it with some sauces and spices.

"What brings you blue folks to these parts?"

Demetris answered, "We were coming to Chathair to get visas to explore further inland."

"No visa needed now."

Grim seemed as comfortable in the wild as in the city. He didn't really seem affected by the loss from the battle at Chathair. Moon grabbed Hanno's hand and they went for a walk toward the pools.

"Where inland?"

"La Venta or what used to be La Venta. We are looking for a cave. A historical site."

"There's a city called Olmec near the three finger cities just north of here. Near there is a small village near Olmec called Venta."

"Do you have a map?"

Grim pulled from a satchel a thick multi bound notebook. The notebook was made of thin sheets of sea rock with carvings and writings on it. He thumbed through the pages to review it.

Moon and Hanno swam in one of the larger pools overlooking a waterfall that easily could have span ten football fields. Moon sat with her chin resting on her palms on the falls side. Hanno swam up to her right, but then used one of his tentacles to tap her on her left shoulder from far on the other side of her.

"Stop don't."

"I'm sorry, just playing what's wrong?"

"Hanno do you think my family will ever change?"

"What do you mean?"

"We used to have happy times you know."

Hanno put his arm around her back, "I know, you miss them don't you?"

"I miss the good times. That thing, that Jelly somehow pulled from me a memory of a perfect day I had with my family. It made me miss them so."

A single tear fell from her eye. Hanno caught it with his other hand.

"I'm sorry we come from such different worlds."

She smiled funny, "Yeah literally different worlds."

He got it and smiled too.

She was honestly unsure how he would answer, "What are we going to do if we find this cyclone storm? Are you going to go back to your world?"

"I don't know. Demetris and Deyva seemed convinced that I'm the key to helping our people return home. But this is my home now too."

"I'm not very happy with my family right now and their judgmental beliefs about grounders let alone their beliefs about sea folk?"

Right then Deyva walked up and jumped in to the pool.

"Oh they knew about us Luas and cast us out of their world thousands of years ago."

Moon turning to Deyva for answers, "Do you think there will ever be a way for us to live together?"

"Some people are so blinded by their own world view that they miss the blessing in God's wonder and creation."

The sun was setting, the pools and waterfalls lit up with golden rainbows in every direction. Grim and Demetris walked up too and just joined the group and took in the wonderful view. They all praised their God for his creation.

The Malrac scout sub passed the blue Caribbean shallow waters and entered the Sigsbee Abyssal Plain and the dark sea bottom. From high above the ocean a flying battle cruiser for New Atlanta held its position. From the ships bridge there was a full complement of shipmates all busy with different assignments. In the center, the Captain and the second were looking over a virtual screen that came up out of a circular electronic map at the center of the bridge. It showed the whole over view of the area included the sea geography.

"Zoom in on the Malrac Sub."

Target and item identifications came up on the screens tactical A.I. The sub was marked and then highlighted showing is tech specs. It included its defensive and assaultive capabilities. The sea floor topography was highlighted and identified with different gulls and valleys labeled as the smart map was moved and adjusted.

Then the A.I. map spoke out, "Unidentified anomaly detected."

All of the other items in view were projected

on the map in great detail as if we were looking at a mini 3d version in real time. But this anomaly was a black hole blob with no shape or definition.

Captain spoke out, "What is that, can we enhance it?"

His navigator was adjusting the map with electronic virtual controls, "Pinging CONSPICs in the area."

"Is it a landslide or maybe volcanic activity?" The image did look like a large side of a sea mountain moving.

"Repositioning Regional DMA and adjusting deep water to Megacycle."

The image was moving toward the sub. And the sub appeared unaware of the massive dark mass. As the image enhanced on the map it started to take shape. It was a massive creature.

"What is that?"

The navigator made some more adjustments and the A.I. then answered, "No known species match. Unidentified life form."

The beast was not completely clear but it now had the appearance of a giant man with wings. It had massive arms and legs but something on its back that resembled wings or fins. Its head and face were not clear.

Inside the sub, the Malrac captain was watching the front view as they approached the landing near the large city gates. Then their own ship logistics picked up the movement, but it was too late.

From the view of the New Atlanta ship the beast was moving on the sub deep under sea.

"Captain should we warn the Mal..."

His request died in his mouth while the image of the beast took over the sub and completely consumed it. This time when the beast turned the sub was visible in its mouth. The massive beasts face was filled with long dark tentacles that help feed the meal of ship and its occupants. Then in an instant the sub and the beast were gone.

The next morning the small band of explorers were packing up their gear. They started out on a hike over the green fields of the Plyacades. The area was up on a plateau. There was a huge wide river on the east side that fed the waterfalls. But on the West side was a Temple. They had walked for several hours and Moon's feet were starting to hurt. She stopped and sat on a rock.

"Hanno doesn't your feet hurt?"

"No not really."

He lifted up his foot and on the bottom he had adjusted his skin to be hardened scales which closely resembled his suckers and hooks of his tentacles.

"No fair, can you all do that."

Demetris and Deyva just nodded but kept walking.

Grim smiled, "My feet are always tough. Don't worry young lady we will be back in the sea soon. They crested the hill and then started back down a steep mountain. When they encountered the sea, it was at waist deep for several miles with long grasses. But at least the seafloor was easier on Moon's feet. The ground then came to a steep cliff that went deep into the ocean for half a mile. But then the group stopped. The slope turned vertical and went straight down. A steep sea cliff rose up on two sides. The whole area was a crevice that span several miles in length but was only twenty feet wide. Between the crevice was a deep underwater gorge. On their side was a manmade or rather Dacacian-made vertical shaft attached to the cliff.

Grim elaborated, "This is the trench ladder. The currents between the sea cliffs can be very strong. The ladder is to help keep us safe as we descend. Don't be afraid to use the rails and sides to help you."

Immediately they felt what he was telling them. Currents were moving and ripping in both direction forcefully from side to side but also up and down. They took their time descending. Grim used his four hands and also his feet which had opposable toes to allow for a good grip. The three Luas were best equipped, using all of their tentacles and two hands to move down. They were the most centered and moved fluidly. Moon was having the most problems and Hanno used more of his Boya to help hold her in the center of the structure as she swam. The ladder looked more like a steel mining elevator shaft but just the framework. It was mostly open allowing the currents to flow through allowing the resistance on the structure to a minimum.

Moon got grabbed by a strong current and her small frame was pulled out of the structure out in the middle of the crevice.

"Wow...Hanno help!"

He lunged two tentacles out after her and grabbed her by the leg. Demetris and Deyva were too far below them to help. She was dangling by her leg in the current. Out of a dark hole on the other side of the cliff a crab like creature slowly started reaching toward her while holding onto the opposite cliff. Moon was dangling with her arms and hair flowing with the current. The crabs claws and feelers were tasting and testing her hair. Moon felt something and looked up and screamed right as Hanno pulled her back with force right into his arms.

"There you are."

Grim just said, "Watch the crunchies they will eat anything, even little Moon."

They moved slowly and carefully. Moon even filled with the bright golden Plava of Hanno all around her felt the change in temperature. It was getting colder than she had ever felt. And even though she was seeing through the Plava she also noticed the deep darkness of the sea cliff as they got closer to the bottom. At about a mile off the sea floor the two sea cliffs opened up. Here the current was dispersed and lighter. But it was pitch black. Grim sparked a sea crystal that was attached to belt and it lit up the area. Now with the Plava she saw a whole new world. He then sparked a few more and handed them out. Deyva, Demetris, and Hanno strapped them to their sword belts on their chests. Moon held hers in her hand. The glow from the crystals created light bubbles around the five travelers. Many beast hovered on the edges in the dark as if they might be hurt by the light. Then they moved as the bubble moved. Dark ancient creatures big and small from both earth and Syrena moved and swam. As they stepped out of the opening of the crevice Moon from her vantage point at the back large dark creatures with sharp rock like backs move out of Grims way as his light moved across the floor. The others saw it too but recognized a threat and pulled their weapons. As Moon left the opening she now saw them better. They were Datos, lots of them. The adults were twenty to thirty feet in length. They were thick and had deep sharp scales and winged fins on their backs. But there were also many juveniles the size of a man's leg. They all scattered and hid from the light.

Grim didn't pull his bow and just said, "Datos are scaredy cats, and go good with peppers." Demetris and Deyva were still cautious and Demetris switched from swords to his gun as they moved along the floor. Now Moon and Hanno were side by side following the others. As her fear subsided over the Datos she now saw the beauty. She saw a small school of fish that were blue with black lines and orange horns and ten orange feathered tails. Then there was a small squid looking creature with squirrel like ears and instead of tentacles he looked like he was floating on small blanket of appendages. And light pulsated through the appendages. When seeing Moon he swam off and joined a group of hundreds similar to him. Then a medium size beast swam up to her crystal looking at it like it was trying to determine if it was some sort of food. The creature had two arms and two legs but fins on the end of all four appendages. He had a round head with large blue eyes. Off the back of his head were long feelers that looked like dreadlocks but he used them to feel and taste the crystal. Moon shook the crystal and spooked him away. Many other beautiful and unique creatures she saw as they moved away from the great sea trench.

CHAPTER 17:
LA VENTA

Rising up off the deep sea floor was a slow rising plateau in the distance. The group had traveled all day and decided to make camp before continuing on. Grim and Hanno gathered up very specific rocks and sea clumps and built what looked like a fire pit. Moon again was so amazed at how the sea folk lived underwater. Moon sort of followed Hanno copying him and thought she was gathering the same type of items. One of the sea clumps she had in her right hand, suddenly opened its eyes and then wiggled free and swam away. She smiled and then followed him. Demetris and Deyva were also scavenging but they were collecting sea moss and sea weed putting them in pouches attached to their waist. Demetris pulled one of his swords and cut down several large columns of kelp. They bunched them and tied them carrying them over their shoulders as they walked. The kelp floated behind them as they moved.

"D what are we going to do if we found the

path but Hanno doesn't want to take it?"

"If we find it, it is once again prophecy fulfilled. It will be a clear sign that he is the one. I would do anything to help the one open the door."

"Don't say that, anything."

Demetris just looked into her eyes and she knew he meant it. When they got back to the fire pit they used the kelp to make seats and chairs. Moon plopped down on hers. She had never been so comfortable. Grim sparked several crystals and the fire erupted. It gave off light and also intense heat.

"Anyone wants some Conger?"

Grim held up a large sea eel seven feet in length. All the men licked their lips as he started roasting it. Deyva handed Moon some moss and seaweeds and several other items that resembled nuts.

"Nice sea salad I'm down."

She thanked Deyva and they all shared a sense of relief as they spoke and ate. Grim pulled from his back a seashell that was covered with a membrane. He popped it and took a swig. Then passed it to his companions. All but Hanno and Moon seemed to know what it was. When Hanno looked at it up close, there was something clearly swimming inside. He popped the top and drank. His Lua side loved it and drank it down. Then it was Moon's turn.

"Go ahead give it a try."

"What's it taste like."

Grim answered, "Like victory young lass."

She popped and then sucked. She coughed and choked and some of it leaked out and turned the sea brown.

"ehhh it taste like salty underwear!"
They all shared a laugh. And when the laughter calmed down they all just starred at the glowing crystals. The mystic underwater deep blue flames moved with the sea like an old friend.

Grim took another swig. Then from deep down in his long throat he sang.

As the Sun's long stretched arms pull back and away; the shadows of the deep stretch out their legs. We sit amidst the long lost streams and start to hear them cry.

Cry ol spirits of the lost.

Cry ol spirits of the warriors past.

Cry ol spirits of the daughters and the sons.

We drift on the long powerful streams; her hair stretches forth and encircles the world. She is powerful and true as a newborn's mother. She holds us up and takes us to good seas full of spender. But we still hear them cry.

Cry ol spirits of the lost.

Cry ol spirits of the warriors past.

Cry ol spirits of the daughter and the sons.

We smell the horizon. We see the slow streams of good seas. She brings us to seas full of spender. We form pairs and we build our homes. But we still hear them cry.

Cry ol spirits of the lost.
Cry ol spirits of the warriors past.
Cry ol spirits of the daughter and
the sons.

Moon was asleep by the third verse. She snuggled next to Hanno and dreamed of strange creatures both kind and dangerous.

The next morning they were up early. While on their journey they mixed between swimming and walking. Slowly growing on their horizon was a bright orange and red glow. It was so bright that it outshone all that was behind it. Then it came into full view. There was a massive undersea lava vent that flowed from east to west as far as the eye could see like a river.

Grim turned to the group, "La Venta."
There were two stone statues planted on each side of the entrance. They stood tall as warnings to those considering crossing the bridge. Each unique but both looking like great sea beasts, half lion and half shark. The great bridge stretched over the lava flow. The bridge started miles before the river and rose up high over it. Although the lava clung to the seafloor; there was fire bubbles and bursts all around. At about the midpoint of the bridge, the city came into view. On the city side of the bridge was a large stone church with two towers. And standing over the church was a huge sea serpent made of stone. The city looked old and gothic. Moon's eyes were wide open as she fascinated at she was seeing. She then heard

a large explosion and looked over the edge of the bridge to investigate. But just before her head cleared the side, Grim lunged and grabbed her with both lower hands.

"Careful little buddy."

Then they all saw it. Great streams of heated sea flowing up from both sides of the bridge. Yet the bridge protected them. Coming down on the city side they saw that La Venta was abandoned. Cursed and forsaken years and years ago. They turned north and found themselves on a stone paved walkway. The walkway had paths above and below separated by twenty feet.

"Grim what's that for?" Moon pointing to the upper walkway.

With one move Grim jump swam and then was walking upside down on the upper walkway.

"For busy pedestrian traffic."

He playfully walked past the other companion's surprising Hanno. Moon laughed at him. At the end of the street was a temple built into the side of a mountain. Its entrance was through a large opening resembling a cave. They sparked crystals and made their way through the cave. There was carvings and drawings of Dacacians, Luas, and even ancient men. At the end of the long cave was a vault chamber. At the center of the chamber was a stone the size of two men but one Dacacian. The stone was rough but also carved.

Deyva was scanned it with her Boya, "It's the hero Twins alright."

The others were walked around it. There was a source of light in the chamber from high. But it was still very dim. Grim was standing guard and not as interested as the others.

"La Venta was one of those cities how do so say, 'sumergido en el mar."

Moon was running her fingers along the designs, "Hanno these are your markings here." Hanno joined at her side.

"D look each Hero appears to be holding a baby."

He too was using his Boya, "Its Hunahpu and Xbalanque. One is from Xibalba and the other from the Jaguar Sun during the blood moon many cycles ago."

Grim just said nonchalantly, "Dacacians fought with the Mayans. Good warriors but small little suckers. Then we found it more useful to make a covenant with them. But the Spaniards were another matter. We ended up returning to the sea until the sea swallowed up the land again."

Hanno asked, "How old are you Grim."

"A warrior never tells his age."

But he said it was like an older refined lady, then he caught Moon's eye. She smiled playfully. Hanno was a little clueless.

Deyva moved around the side, "Here look Syrena markings."

They all moved closer. When Hanno approached, his golden Boya Plava lit up. A more correct observation was the Stone drew from him his Boya like a stream of light from Hanno to the stone. It was so intense it ripped his shirt and the markings on his chest moved and changed. Moon had seen him move and transform his tentacles but had never seen his body change in this way. It was like the stone was moving a cypher built into his markings.

Deyva followed his Boya from the stone to his chest, "D look it's changing."
She quickly pulled from her pack the device from her study and was using it to analysis the changes. The connection to the stone via his Boya was creating so much energy that it was lifting him off the floor. Then suddenly a large clap and pop and the light was gone. Hanno was knocked out, floating unconscious. Moon and Demetris who were closest lightly guided him down to their waist high and were checking on him. Deyva then came closer too and checked his vitals.

"He appears Ok."

Demetris now getting a closer look at his chest, "This changes everything."

Deyva working the device, "We have new coordinates."

Moon worried looking to the two adult Luas for guidance, "What does this mean?"
Demetris and Deyva looked at her.

Demetris then said, "We have the coordinates to the passage..."

Deyva finished for him, "Our passage back home."

Moon asked, "Don't we still need a storm or cyclone thingy?"
Deyva and Demetris look at her, then to each other, then back to Hanno.

They spent two days swimming and hiking out of the city of La Venta, back over the lava bridge, and then across the vacant plains. Every step felt heavier as they approached the deep, dark trench. Its one thing to cross the plains looking toward the bright light of the lava river. It is something else walking toward the deep, dark trench. You might ask yourself why they couldn't just swim up at an angle from the bridge to the top of the trench. Dacacians and Luas were not the greatest beasts of the sea. And many horrible and dangerous beasts roamed these waters. It would be like asking a safari guide why he didn't just take the tour group along the Mara River banks in Kenya. One misstep and you fall into a river full of alligators. Or one step the other and you walk into a pride of hungry lions. Grim was guiding them through the safest passage he knew. It was also the trading route for this region when La Venta was thriving and full of Dacacians. With each step toward the trench, they all felt something evil, something powerful. Whether it was fate or fear they all felt it. They arrived at the trench gate and started heading up the long ladder toward the top. Then without warning, a large shadow moved behind them. Grim stop leading the group and motioned them to pass him.

He grabbed with his feet two rungs on opposite sides. Then his massive leg muscles expanded as he slowly lowered his body and drew his massive bow. His eyes locked on the darkness. Moon's fear was rising as she saw Grim taking his position. She pulled on Hanno who was helping her navigate the ladder. Now everyone could saw Grim and came to a stop. Demetris pulled his large sidearm. Grim slowly pulled from his large quiver an arrow with a crystal tip. He sparked it and then launched it. The group watched the shining arrow as it flew through the dark sea. Then it impacted what at first looked like a huge rock, but it suddenly moved. And it was moving fast right at them. Then Grim shouted, "MOVE!"

It was not clear to anyone but Grim the level of threat they were under. The side of a mountain moved after them. The mountain that chased them was a Cthulhu, known to locals as Jimbo. An evil all-consuming beast. And they were the next on his menu. The Luas exploded with energy using both Boya and kinetic grabbing and swinging with all of their tentacles up the ladder. Deyva's Boya was extended and surrounded them like a shield. Demetris and Hanno's Boya mixed and made the most unique green energy surge moving Moon up with force. They flipped her between each other as they grabbed moved and shot at the beast. Jimbo stretched out his mountain sized arm and hand towards the structure. Grim now was also moving and shooting the large Dacacian arrows. But they had no affect.

Smash, crash, Jimbo's hand crushed three stories of ladder with one swipe. They were moving so fast now. He then shot up his other arm taking out four more stories. But the trench fortunately was too narrow for his biceps and they were just out of reach. So he forced his massive disgusting face into the trench. The sides of his head through rocks in all directions. They pushed forward. Now with Jimbo's head wedged in the cliff, his face unfurled his tentacles each one fifty to seventy feet in length. They slithered and reached up through the openings of the ladder. Deyva turned her body while still using her tentacles to climb upward. She moved her arms and hands to form a pattern and then a formula conjuring a powerful Boya weapon. Once it was formed she shot it right at the eyes of the beast. The blue Boya hit him square between the eyes and for a moment he froze stunned. But not as long as she hoped. Demetris was shooting his energize gun as he moved. The beasts scales were too thick. Jimbo brought down his fists in frustration and pounded the cliff. A giant junks of rock broke loose and fell into the trench. The impact caused Hanno to lose his grip on Moon and she fell out of the ladder and was caught up in the current of the trench. The tentacles of the Cthulhu stretched through the openings in the cracks of the landslide rocks like eerie tongues. They grabbed Moon on her legs and then pulled her.

"Moon!"

All four jumped out of ladder grabbing at her arms and body. Grim dropped down on the cluster of rocks that formed across the trench from the debris and pulled two swords one for each of his two right hands. He sliced at the monstrously thick tentacles as the others pulled her free. Then the remaining tentacles of the beast disappeared. They didn't stop to think but just moved on as fast as they could. They made it to the top of the ladder and out of the trench. Looking back there appeared no way the beast could fit through the narrow trench. They were still in the sea but at the slow rising slope with hundreds of feet of sea over their heads.

"Is everyone ok?" Deyva asked.

"Other than almost being eaten, yeah I guess." Moon still had her sense of humor.

Hanno was holding her hand so tightly she had to get his attention, "I'm Ok you can let go now."

She had slight sucker sores on her arm from his grip. She was rubbing it and looking around. Demetris still had his gun out and then he holstered. Grim too put his swords away.

Grim to Demetris, "Did you see that, my arrows are going to give him a headache for a day or two. Better than that little peashooter of yours."

Demetris could leave it unanswered, "Peashooter, I'll have you know that this Arma de foc was handed down to me from the ancient order of Senusret Royal Navy. It is designed with unlimited utanir energy ammo that is self-guided and targeted by my Boya eyesight. It has been known to split a Lusca at forty meters."

Grim rubbed his chin, "Well for a Royal de foc whatever you called it, Jimbo didn't seem to even notice."

Hanno and Moon were enjoying the two warriors boasting over the battle. Then their faces froze in fear. From over the other side of the trench cliff the Cthulhu rose up and now could be seen in the full light of the lit sea. Standing fifteen stories tall with arms of a man, head of a squid and face full of now clearly seen hundreds of tentacles. Out of his scaly back two full body sized winged fins. He flapped his fins and stretched out his arms. His whole body was filled with dark green scales armored and powerful. There was nothing they could do. Nowhere they could go. His hands and long green claws came right at them.

POPPOPPOPPOP BOOM BOOM BOOOM!!!!
Fifty explosions happened at once, at multiple locations, all over the beast. Then again another volley of explosions. The bursts exploded the water pushing them twenty feet up the rise. The explosions continued without interruption. The beast turned its attention toward the sky as if it could launch a counter attack, but the barrage was so great all it could do was receive more damage. Then a glowing burst that Demetris recognized

as a Battleship nuclear energy torpedo. It hit the water and then really accelerated.

"Keep moving, keep moving up the hill!"

The torpedo entered the water at the perfect moment in between the bursts and struck Jimbo square on the top of his head. This explosions exploded outward and upward in bright blue and white. It sent shock waves in every direction knocking fifty feet or more. When the sea dust settled Jimbo's head was only a few meters from them and was cracked wide open with green ooze pouring into the sea. Instantly twenty New Atlanta battle cruisers entered in from the surfaces above them and security personnel swarmed everywhere in tactical underwater suits. While everyone was still in shock they grabbed up Moon and Hanno. Demetris, Deyva, and Grim were able to escape into the shadows of the sea.

CHAPTER 18: INTO THE BELLY OF DESPAIR

Moon was led by several guards to the outer deck of a massive command cruiser hovering over the dark blue waters. Hundreds of feet below were spiking cliffs jutting out of the sea from where the area of Baja California used to be. Hanno was there in shackles Moon went straight to him and hugged him. Lord Cadel came from a side door from the bridge.

"Happy to see him but not your own father who rescued you?"

She turned but stayed by Hanno's side. Several guards tried to separate them but Cadel waved them off. Denton was nearby and wasn't going to have another near escape. He moved closer to the two.

"Daddy why is he a prisoner?"

Cadel moved while he talked looking out over the edge of the ship down at the sea.

"The real question is, why have you chosen

sea folk over your own kind?"

She shot back, "I love him Daddy, I.."

He interrupted, "What this..this. squid on two legs. What are you even talking about?"

She tried to respond but her father continued, "The Order has taught us that these beasts are lower evolved beasts. That they are not men but fish that belong to the sea."

All she could get out was, "Daddy."

But this time it came with a forfeiting cry.

He stood tall and proud, "Bliss IX 22 states 'The mind of the sea folk are full of foolish thoughts of gods and magic and are not considered to be intellectual and thus forth they shall not mix marry or mate with any member of the Order of Bliss nor any human.' You know Moon I once saw a half breed and he was hideous, living amongst the rocks at the bottom of the bay eating sea slugs and crabs."

This was in fact a common New Atlanta rumor that actually was not a sea folk but a creature that had come over with the sea folk from Syrena known as an Akula. He finally paused and grabbed the rails looking out over the view. He had done this many times at their home looking over the city when he would school her.

Moon approached him, "Daddy I do miss you and mother, and even Body if you can imagine that."

That soften him some.

"But daddy is there anything that can be

done?"

He didn't answer.

"Could I move? I don't have to live in New Atlanta. I could move to the beach."

As she tried to plead with him offering up one suggestion after another his gaze was fixed on the sea. Up between a circle of sea rocks rose a Malrac Sub. The Sub lifted higher until it hovered on level with the command ship. An energy bridge stretched out and connected the two battleships. A dark door opened on the sub and out came Baron Blavalotski and several of his guardians. When she saw it, her words fell from her mouth. The New Atlanta security guards moved Hanno across the bridge. She ran to him. Denton snatched her. The two young lovers gazed into each other's eyes one last time. Then he disappeared into the darkness of the sub. Which then sunk back into the sea. Moon burst into tears. The weight of it all completely crushed her. Denton handed her off to two several guards that carried her away. Cadel moved back into the bridge and the ship readjusted its positioning preparing for journey back to New Atlanta. From down in the sea, Demetris and Deyva were looking up from under the surface as Nerwin was pulling up in the Cheonia.

Deep in the command sub of Blav, Hanno was tied and stretched out over an examination table. His legs were harnessed with special straps, so that even changing shape did nothing. Blav entered as several Dacacians and Malrac doctors were poking, prodding, and evaluating his chest and markings.

Blav asked, "What kind of progress have you made?"

A skinny smaller Malrac stepped forward, "Your excellence we have the coordinates. It is in the Azores Island chain near Sao Miguel Island."

Back on the Cheonia Demetris and Deyva were in the galley at the table. Deyva was empowering her device with her Boya as it displayed the scan of Hanno.

Deyva zooming in, "That makes so much sense."

"What does?"

"It's at Atlantis."

She was moving and adjusting the scan.

"Azores is east of Gibraltar. According to Cosmas Indicopleustes, also known as Cosmas the Monk, a Greek merchant who wrote of Atlantis in his Christian Topography. He talked about the famous battle of the Delta between the Egyptians and the famous 'sea peoples."

Demetris finally tracking in, "Oh Insula Atlas."

"Right Island of Atlas, Archeons city."

Nerwin waddled into the galley handing both of them drinks, "Who is Archeon?"

Demetris answered, "Well good sir your logs may have recordings of the mythological city of Atlantis that fell into the sea. But the Island of Atlas was the first underwater settlements of the

Luas. Archeon was a corporal second class on our ship. He and other survivors made a trade port near the entrance to the Mediterranean."

Deyva added, "Well before it was destroyed by battle. But the legend of the underwater city lived on."

Deyva turned to the designs illuminating from the device, "Makes sense that the worm hole was near the first settlement."

Demetris countered, "But we had looked here for centuries and found nothing."

Deyva pulled back the scan showing Hanno, "That's before we found him."

Back on the Malrac sub, Blav was yelling at the doctor, "Are you sure you can open the portal?"

The smaller Malrac had long, red, spiked tentacle appendages that better resembled long slender crab claws. He started poking at the markings. We can feel the pain in Hanno's face. Hanno was strapped down and his mouth and eyes were covered.

The doctor continued, "I believe with the right motivation we can activate his..energy source..what do they call it?"

He was looking to his younger staff, "Poya blav something or other."

Blav turned and stepped the short distance to the subs bridge, "Very good."

Then to his communication officers, "Execute Operation Bliksem!"

The southern district of New Atlanta was

the naval port of the city. Lord Cadel's command ship was pulling up to the port. Here only VIP's and military ships were allowed to dock. Moon was in a well-furnished room but under lock and key. She lay in the corner still wearing her "battle suit" that Deyva had given her. The room was completely dark. She was barely visible in the far corner. In the distance the sounds of the ship making ready for port could be heard.

Silently she whispered, "God I know I haven't ever called on you. I do believe in you. I've seen you in the beautiful skies of New Atlanta. I've heard your soft voice in the waves of the sea. And in these last few amazing weeks I've experienced your creative power and love in my discovery of the sea folk. Lord, you know how much my heart aches. Oh Lord, I miss Hanno. It's like a piece of my heart has been ripped from me. But I miss my family too. I pray for you to be my God. Only you can do the impossible."

As she said "impossible", she slumped deeper into the corner now with her head completely on the ground.

"How can we be together? My father will never let us live at peace. Please save my soul. Save my sweet Hanno's life and make a way for us to be together."

Then silence and soft whimpering.

The massive ship slowed, and beams of energy pulled and connected as thousands of dock hands prepped the arrival. Off to the East flashes of hot bright lights flashed from far way. Like small sunbursts that spanned the whole length of New Atlanta.

Lord Cadel was in command, "Denton can you and your agents assist with getting Moon aboard my transport?"
Before Denton could give a 10-4, the control screens lit up with activity.

"T.A.C. contact bearing 10.9.13, multiple tangos."

"Copy T.A.C., subsurface do you copy?"

"Substat copies multiple tangos...tango tango tango, fireflies inbound."

Cadel stepped up, "Evasive maneuvers, take us back out and to a safe position."

"Copy CIC helm defensive alpha two twenty zeta."
The ship quickly broke contact with the dock and started pulling away. From the dock screen Cadel could see Mrs. Cadel and Brodie standing with other families of the crew completely unaware of the impending attack.

"Commander we are not the primary target and should be able to break free."
Moon felt the huge ship move and she slid across the floor.

"Commander Target Alpha is New Atlanta..."
And before he could respond, an array of multiple beam torpedo's impacted the underside of the city causing massive explosions. The bright blue and

green energy that held up the city shot out bright then went dark. Several explosions were close to the port and exploded outward causing massive damages to the command ship. The city seemed to stand completely still like a heavy anvil balancing on a pin, then suddenly started moving at an angle with a great amount of force toward the Atlantic Ocean. All throughout the city, the buildings that were held up by the energy technology were crashing down into the streets then crashing toward the now sliding end of the city. Explosions were everywhere. As the city fell, a line of Malrac warships could be seen moving off into the distance.

The command ship had not completely been released from the docking beams and was being forcefully pulled down with the city as it fell. Moon was flung up and smacked into the ceiling. Then thrown toward the wall. Then the ship exploded and broke apart. The whole ship broke into pieces and was falling with the debris from the falling city. The ship fell slightly ahead of the city. Large junks of the cities machinery and cracked foundation fell all around them. Moon's state room broke apart too opening up to the chaos. She was falling with pieces of her room looking up as a massive city heating coil that was only ten feet above her. She knew she had to get out of the ship and fall free from it. She started climbing up the side of the wall grabbing on to furniture and walls. She climbed slow at first but then gained ground. Right as she grabbed the top her room, the ship fell out from below her. She was now free falling. She moved through the air pushing and pulling at anything she could get her hands on. For a moment she fantasied about having tentacles like Hanno. Off on the far end of the debris was a cable line. She reached out for it but it was just out of reach. At one point you could see a slight blue energy start to form from near her chest. It was Hanno's energy that she somehow still contained. The energy reached out and pulled her and the cable together. She grabbed it with both hands and then pulled forcefully. She flew away from a wall of massive falling wreckage. And when she flew, she appeared to even soar a little on the Boya. Then she flipped and lined up and splashed down feet first into Open Ocean. Moon fell deeper and deeper into the sea. As she sunk she looked up on the destruction. First large chunks of her father's ship fell into the sea but fell to the right and the left of her. She sank deeper. Then a huge debris field of pieces of the docking port and the cities fell all around her, barely missing her. She was frozen in fear, despair, and shock as she sunk with the debris. Then a huge splash when the city itself crashed down into the sea. And even though it was off in the distance she felt the massive rush of water like a tidal wave. It pushed her towards the open ocean. She sunk even deeper.

Deep in the darkness a small glow of blue Boya emitted from around Moon. It was weakening and slowly began to fade. Moon fell into the deep darkness of the quiet dark ocean. The darkness swallowed her whole. In the darkness, she felt a slick warm pink all around her. Then a sharp poke to her chest. Disoriented she shook it off and began to fall back into death.

Poke, Poke, Poke!

This time it poked her out of the grave.

She cried out, "What on Poseidon's butt are you doing?"

Moon opened her eyes and all around her was pink and grey. And everything was wet and sticky. Her eyes focused on a large creature standing over her holding what was clearly a poking stick. The creature was tall maybe seven feet in height. It had four legs which it stood upright on and four arms. But not arms and legs at all. The beast better resembled a cricket or maybe a shrimp but definitely of the Grylloidea family. Its legs had two joints that bent. One bent forward and one backward. Its body was made of an exoskeleton with a hard spiky shell that was green in color on the front and white on the back. It had two arms that were as long as its legs with only one joint. But then a second set of arms that were short and close to the chest and only long enough to reach its mouth. Its head was armored but also human like. And atop of its head was two long antenna that were soft and stretched down its back like two ponytails. That should have been her first clue. Moon stood quickly and surveyed her surroundings. The creature attempted to talk to her but she heard.

"Click, quork, click, click, snap, crunch."

"Where am I?"

"Click, snap, snap, click."

She looked and quickly realized she was inside what looked like a large stomach or mouth.

"Eeww gross, are we inside someone's stomach?"

The beast reached out its staff and touched the top which appeared to have some sort of device. It then touched the device to Moons chest. Then she heard her.

"I am Karkalec, you are welcome to my home who is Balene."

Moon heard a deep wise older female's voice.

"You are a female?"

The giant shrimp cricket nodded yes.

"And where are we?"

"We are in Balene."

"What or who is Balene."

"Balene is my friend and companion."

"Yeah but what is she?"

"Oh Balene is an, what do you call them, I guess she is like your Antarctic Blue Whale but bigger."

Right then Balene moved and Moon fell down. But Karkalec who was very stable with her four double segmented legs only moved slightly.

Karkalec began to excitedly rub her two smaller arms together in excitement.

"Dinner time."

A rush of water flooded the gut and on it a load of giant krill floated in. Karkalec went to work scurrying around grabbing and eating the krill before it continued down the gullet.

Karkalec extended a handful, "Are you hungry?"

"Um I'm good."

As Moon sat on the slippery tongue of the massive beast we now see Balene as she swam out to sea.

CHAPTER 19:
THE PATH LEADS
TO HOPE

Distance, in the Open Ocean, can be a hard thing to measure. Vila Franca do Campo is a small town on the southern part of the island of Sao Miguel. Sao Miguel Island was a part of a string of islands known as the Azores Island chain. Sao Miguel is often thought of as being associated with Europe and Portugal specifically. When in fact it is thousands of miles from any major land mass. Sao Miguel is approximately fifteen hundred miles from St. Johns Newfoundland to the West. Eighteen hundred miles away from Nanortalik Greenland to the North. And nine hundred miles from Lisbon Portugal to the East. And lastly three thousand miles away from the recently crumbled remains of New Atlanta. To Moon it might as well be on the other side of the planet. This distance was one the reasons they were able to survive the Great War. But distance wasn't the only reason. Many other factors helped too. The islands vast array of self-sustaining agriculture; their ability to live of the fruits of the sea; and the abundance of fresh water. The islands unique geography has many volcanically formed freshwater lakes, high mountains and lush meadows. When nuclear bombs struck the continents, the sea currents and the climate kept fallout from far from them. When the world starved and fought over scraps, they lived off the seas and their crops. When the world fell under the changing climate. Their climate held tight. So when the great floating cities rose into the skies they were all surprised to find Sao Miguel thriving. Some would say the islands were blessed. It is here in these blessed islands the Cheonia has arrived. Demetris was out of his chair and at a side control station.

"Nerwin slow to ten knots all stations go zero ten dark."

Nerwin was at a lower forward part of the bridge. It had a built in station similar to his back charging dock near the galley but this one allowed him to run the ship from the bridge. Deyva took her seat at the bridge and was helping.

"Power controls are dark captain."

"Good bring her in nice and easy."

The Cheonia was pulling up to Vila do Porto Archipelago. It was sixty two miles south of Vila Franca do Campo. Deyva looking and adjusting the screens to show a tactical map of Campo.

"The islands shadow is hiding us from their sensors."

"Great."

Demetris takes his seat at the Captain's chair.

"Send out Staci."

Nerwin responded, "Sending out Staci, go girl fly with the currents."

Nerwin said it with so much sass, you could almost hear his heavy weighted hand snap. Staci or rather S.T.A.C.I. Strategic Tactical Autonomous Combat Intelligence drone launched from the bottom of the Cheonia. Staci looked more like a sea turtle underwater then it did a drone. She swam deep and smooth toward Vila Franca do Campo. Multiple sensor feeds from Staci pushed back to the Cheonia giving them data on nautical conditions, sea temperature, currents, and sonar of ships, geography, and all the sea life in the area. She flew low along the seafloor. She flew down a slope and then back up again. When she topped a sea cliff the sensors lit up.

Nerwin calmly, "Captain multiple contacts, checking."

Deyva and Demetris were active in their adjusting and analyzing data as Nerwin searched. Deyva and Demetris said under their voice what Nerwin confirmed.

"Multiple battle cruisers. Check affiliation."

This time D and D answered for him, "Malrac's."

Nerwin confirmed, "Yes sir."

Deep inside of Balene, Moon was inside a strange looking shack resting in a hammock. The shack was made of boat parts, wood, and nets with ropes everywhere. Moon was slowly being rocked by the swimming movements of Balene. Karkalec was sitting in a larger chair that was attached to the side of the shake. The shack was built into the flesh of the massive whale's insides. There was a soft glow coming off of some sea crystals inside the shack. Karkalec was cleaning her mandibles with her short busy little arms and claws. Even a giant Raka from Syrena knows when a human is sad.

"Miss Moon why are you so sad."
Moon turned toward the wall of the shack.

"You don't understand."

"Try me."
She then quickly turned and tried to sit up.

"Oh Ok well let's see. My boyfriend was taken prisoner by what I can only described as a bunch of giant black vampire squids and green lizards looking beasts. Then everyone I ever knew. Basically my whole family was blown up in the attack on New Atlanta. And let's see."
She paused as she lifted her right hand which was dripping with whale saliva.

"And now, I'm floating adrift to God knows where in the belly of a whale. What am I Jonah?"

"I'm so sorry dear. I've have had loss as well. I'm not sure I understand completely, who is Jonah?"

"Never mind."
Moon at first started with a slight whimper but

then fell into a deep sadness and cried deeply. Karkalec rose from her seat and then used her longer arm and softly rubbed Moon's back. She then lowered the light and left the shack.

When Staci arrived at a safe distance, she surfaced. Her back had a shell that also resembled a sea turtle. Several ports on her back opened up and smaller Staci's flew in the air. The Cheonia was now getting these feeds as well.

"Approaching Vila Franca do Campo" Nerwin announced.

They all were captivated by the screen. On the screens were images of the small town. The town was full of Malrac operatives. What Deyva and Demetris had known for some time was that the Malracs had used aggressive propaganda and diplomacy throughout the world but especially on all of the islands states. These political actions had caused them to be well known as trading partners in places that the floating cities would not have thought.

Deyva in disbelief, "They must have read the signs on Hanno."

Demetris just added, "It would appear so."

"Nerwin send Staci to forward target and continue scan."

"Copy that Captain." Then to Staci, "Go my beautiful girl."

Nerwin's computer face image on his circular portal screen had a longing look toward her screen feed.

Demetris turning to Deyva, "They may be here but, have they discovered the gate."

Deyva, "How can you know that?"

"I believe it. This gate was not meant for them."

Staci dove back down into the deep as her flying children were overhead. The small aerial drones were so small they were invisible to sensors. Staci on the other hand had to be more careful. Staci approached Vila Franca Islet. A small vegetated uninhabited islet eighteen hundred feet south of Campo. It was an island that had a Volcanic Cone made of sharp volcanic columns. The cone was dormant but full of seawater. As Staci arrived to the islet, her sensors scanned the islet below the surface of the sea. The cone appeared to go deep down into the sea beyond sensor range. From above Staci's children scanned the surface and it just looks like a floating island with a lake in the middle, but from below there was rich, deep layers of geography and shapes.

"Nerwin bring up the scans and load them into the nanotitan."

Deyva saw something.

"Loaded and ready."

Now Demetris and Deyva looked together. Deyva reached out two of her tentacles toward the front screen. Then manipulates the screen and stretched and brought it closer to them.

"See here do those look like something?"

"Yeah I see it."

Then Deyva to Nerwin again, "Nerwin lock and drop visual layer of aphanitic rocks."

"Lock and drop."

Layers of igneous basalt rock formations disappear from the image of the underwater inverted volcanic stack.

"Enhance Farihao cone at points thirty three to one twenty one."

"Enhanced."

"You see it?"

Both of them looked closely. Then it came into view. The inverted cone that was believed to be of volcanic design now appeared to be manmade or rather Lua made. The structure was full of designs and structural architecture and was clearly some enormous object.

"Is it a ship?"

"I don't know."

"Wait hold on."

Deyva was quick at work. She brought up the scans of Hanno's markings and then overlaid them with the object. Way at the bottom of Hanno's design was a gate and a vortex interwoven in the markings. And at the bottom was the cone.

"This is it. The gate. See the markings. They match early designs by the Shekelesh Luas."

Demetris thinking about what she said, "You mean the Sea People?"

"It has to be our gate."

Moon was up on her feet but her whole body showed her sadness. Her chin was on her chest, her hair was in front of her face. She didn't even notice that Karkalec was sitting on the opposite end watching her. Karkalec was sitting on a small mound of eggs sitting in a concave in the corner of the whale side across from the shack. Moon was walking slow but with intent toward the back of the great beast's throat. Balene was not a whale from this world but from Syrena and Karkalec was in a symbiotic relationship with Balene. Balene provide a safe home and an abundance of food. And Karkalec helped Balene with a number of internal health issues including cleaning unwanted items that somehow find their way into her innards. Moon was barefoot and making deliberately slugging steps on Balene's tongue sloshing the saliva as she moved. Then she reached the edge of the great beast's throat. She was standing so close and looking down into the darkness. The darkness and the sadness seemed to call to her. Karkalec had her four lower limbs at four points over her nest and was grabbing one after another with her smaller appendages rotating them and inspecting them.

Karkalec asked, "You know Balene takes several months to digest her food. I imagine it would be a horribly painful way to die."

"Maybe I deserve to die. What else is there for me?"

Karkalec paused as she held an egg. The little Raka was swimming in the egg sack making very low but sweet high pitched cooing noises.

"Well maybe. But don't you still have a..boy.. or something?"

"Yeah Hanno but he is probably dead by now."

"Probably. That's not very certain. Is he or isn't he um dead."

A Raka thought process were very simple and very yes no oriented. More beast than being. Moon turned to look at her strange new acquaintance.

"Well I'm not sure."

"Why not?"

"Well I am here deep under the sea with no way out. Even if I did somehow survive this how would I find him? How would I get to him? How would I save him?"

Karkalec scratched her spiky chin with her little left hand.

"Well go see."

It was that simple. Try, have faith, have hope. Maybe he was alive. Maybe she could help him. The small simple thought grew in her like a seed of a great tree. Her faith grew.

Moon completely about faced and looked at her strange friend.

"I will."

Right when she was about to take a step Balene moved suddenly and opened her mouth. The movement caused Moon's back foot to slip and she fell. She was holding on to the edge of the giant tongue but it was so slimy and slippery. In and instant Karkalec grabbed her and lifted her up in the air. Then a rush of water and krill rushed in. Karkalec was still holding Moon in the air and her strong arms were pinching Moon. But she was bent forward and away holding Moon behind her as she gobbled up the nourishing treat.

"Um can I get down?"

"Oh sorry hon."

She placed her down. Moon hadn't eaten for days.

"I guess I need my strength up if I plan on getting out of here."

She bent over and was fishing through and was grabbing at the swimming and moving krill. Near one large pile she was about to lift the krill to her mouth and out popped a face.

"What... yikes... is this?"

She stepped back and the face rose up out of the pile of food and it had a body attached to it.

"Well hello my dear I am Edward."

He reached out a large webbed hand and she shook it warily. Edward was a Peixe. Not quite Dacacian but had many similar features. He was about six feet tall, green but instead of the hardened lizard like armor he was soft and smooth with light green scales. He had long flipper like webbed feet and just as long flipper webbed hands. He had soft flowing green fins that ran the length of his back but also down the backside of his legs and arms. His torso looked human enough. On his face were sets of long fins that ran back from his sides and top and looked like hair but were clearly fins. He had a kind face of a man but with what looked like coral growing off his chin.

Karkalec quickly approached Edward, "Oh Eddie how long has it been."

They exchanged some sort of greeting that involved them smacking appendages back and forth that looked like a secret handshake.

"Hey Kark hows it hanging?"

"You know baby roasted can't wait till these littler boogers hatch."

Eddie sat down and was cleaning krill out of from between the claws on his webbed feet. But it really just looked like he was eating some junk out from between his toes.

"Well you know the Samkoma has begun."

Karkalec's energy was instantly infused, "No no I hadn't heard I've been in here nesting for the last several months. Tell me tell me everything."

"The call went out from Hoofdstad, the Lua Capital. But I had seen the signs coming for some time."

"Signs what signs."

Moon stepped into their circle and was now just as interested, "What signs?"

They both looked at her funny but Eddie continued, "Well first there were rumors that a Tanel the tribe of Daihbi had come forward."

Moon turned her head slightly, "Wait I've heard this before."

Eddie continued, "Then Chathair was destroyed by the Malrac's."

Moon couldn't hold back, "I was there I saw it."

"You were there?"

They both wondered who this human was.

"But when the flying enclave crashed into the sea I was sure."

Moon knew he was talking about New Atlanta.

She asked, "Do you know if there were any survivors?"

"Oh sure sure, lots of boats, ships, and planes. Lots and lots of bobbers."

"What are bobbers?"

Karkalec knew to Eddie bobbers were bodies in the water. But she covered slightly for her new friend.

"Oh honey sounds like there are survivors."

"Yeah thanks."

Moon was still trying to wrap her head around the whole thing.

Then Eddie ended with, "But then the call came. The Luas had the pathway to the gate and all residents of Syrena were called to the Somkoma."

Karkalec could see Moon had a question on her face, "It's the great gathering of all the children of Atlas to come and find the way home."

Moon caught it, "Oh path you must be talking about Hanno."

Eddie stood and stretched, "I don't know any Hanno but I know the location of the Somkoma."

Karkalec gave Eddie some sort of high five.

"Ok we are off."

Karkalec made some vibrations and clicks. And Balene changed course heading toward the gate.

CHAPTER 20:
ATLANTIS RISEN

Slowly moving from just over the horizon was an older ship. It moved and swayed on the calm sea. The base of the ship had a single hull that was rusted but sturdy and made from steel. Jutting out from multiple sides of the ship were newer luminescent metals similar to those used in New Atlanta. The sides went out, then up, but then back down to the surface. Each side had a newer pontoon also made from the newer metal. Above these attached pontoon arms were several layers of decks made from a variety of material including wood, metals both old and new. Then over the multilayered decks were sails strung up by ropes used as protection from the sun making the ship look like a very strange pirate or raider ship of some sort. Out the aft were three of the attached pontoons. Attached to the back and bottom of these pontoons were jet engines that looked like they came off of a New Atlanta military flying ship. As the ship got closer it now appeared to actually be traveling quite fast.

On board the Cheonia Nerwin announced, "Captain unidentified Ship approaching to the south."

Demetris turned looking at the back screens, "Enhance image and zoom in."
In the zoomed in view there were a number of occupant's on the ship grounders, sea folk, and New Atlanta survivors. All looked tired, worn, and wounded. Then an even closer scan showed the Cadel family and Detective Denton.

Going back in time just before New Atlanta fell. Moon was back in her room aboard the battle cruise belonging to New Atlanta. Lord Cadel was on the bridge.

"Prepare for docking procedures."

"Aye Aye Commander."

Another shipmate spoke out, "Commander we are getting a 4JG decoded message. It appears to be coming from the suspected Lua ship the Malracs were tracking."

Cadel arrogantly just said, "Ok what's it say."

"Urgent imminent attack, multiple hostiles approaching."

Cadel didn't believe it, "What what do sensors show."

"Sensors are clear sir."
Down deep in the ocean Demetris and Deyva were watching.

Nerwin turned to them, "Alerts received."
Demetris and Deyva had been slowly but cautious following the command cruiser from deep in the

ocean. Hoping to find a moment to free Moon and Hanno. But when they saw the armada of Malracs show up they tried to warn Cadel. But it was too late.

Then the attack and devastation of New Atlanta unfolds before them in slow motion. Lord Cadel was standing in the bridge. The bridge was designed to be better insulated from any attack. The first wave of the attack instantly disabled and also destroyed large portions of the base and the ship.

Cadel yelled out, "Abandoned ship all personal to rescue and evacuation operations!"
Cadel had his eyes locked on the screen of his family Janice and Brody Cadel. They were on the heavily reinforced military dock on the southern end. The closest explosion impacted the forward part of the base which sent a blast of luminescent metals like shrapnel toward the cruiser. The materials low visibility made it seem like the ship and the dock were being struck by invisible weapon fire. A burst of metal severed the whole starboard side of the cruiser exploding and separating Moons whole wing. Cadel ran to the side of the bridge that was now open to the ocean as he watched Moon fall with the debris and rubble.

"Moon, my baby girl!"
Denton grabbed him as Cadel almost went out the opening.

"Commander we have to get you to the

escape pod."

Denton hustled Cadel away and they both ran and jumped into an escape pod. As Cadel sat looking at the interior screens of the pod he saw that Janice and Brody had also managed to escape aboard a ship with a number of airmen at the base. Deep under the ocean the Cheonia searched the area.

"The Malrac fleet has left heading out into the Atlantic."

Deyva nervously searching her systems, "Did you try infrared?

Nerwin answered, "Yes so sign of her."

"What about sonar and DO sensors?"

"Yes nothing." Nerwin then just said, "No signs of any life below the surface."

Off in the distance the bulk of New Atlanta nosed dived down into the Frying Pan Shoals. The shoals were a shallow portion of the Atlantic were sentiment from the Cape Fear River had been built up over thousands of years. The area was also just past what used to be known as Bald Head Island. Of course the island had been flooded for hundreds of years but the shoals persisted. And now was temporarily keeping the city from sinking completely into the depths of the ocean. The massive sized city now with its nose down and end up looked like a great mountain expanding far up into the sky. The Luas that were hiding in the shadows of the sea showed up to help the survivors of New Atlanta. Cadel's Pod landed at a group of vessels. All flying ships had eventually lost power

and were now dead in the sea with other floating
sea ships. They tied all of the surviving ships
together. Luas and human both New Alantian
and Grounders alike worked hand in hand to save
souls. Vincent Cadel was a different man when he
stepped off that escape pod. There was a platform
created that spanned all of the ships. It had
been constructed out of pieces of New Atlanta's
damaged remains. Thousands had made it to the
temporary safety of the ships. Now the secret of
the sea folk was out and the laws of the Order
seemed to be empty concerns. Cadel was moving
among the crowd. Denton followed closely behind.
What remained of the city security and emergency
services were also there attending to the wounded.
And then he saw them and ran to them. Vincent,
Janice, and Brody fell into a family hug. Demetris
and Deyva saw the survivors and there was no sign
of Moon or Hanno.

Demetris touching Deyva's shoulder softly,
"Moon's gone. There's still a chance we can rescue
Hanno from the Malracs."
She nodded silently and they moved off into the
dark.

The scrappy recently constructed ship had
pulled up on the south side of Vila Franca Islet.
The ship slowed and its engines came to a full stop.
The Cheonia sat less than fifty feet below them.

Nerwin, "The ship has pinged us should we
leave stealth mode and respond?"

Deyva to Demetris, "What could they

possibly want?"

"Only one way to see."

The Cheonia rose up from the depths right next to ship. Cadel was on the third deck that was most open and able to receive guests. The Cheonia rose up out of the sea and floated at the same level as the deck. A side door that was invisible before became visible and open up and out creating a platform that connected to the ship. Out came Demetris and Deyva. They were still in tactical gear and also still well armed. Denton still was armed with his powerful energy weapon still strapped across his chest now more visible without his jacket. Neither were anticipating a fight.

Cadel spoke first, "The Order says if a man seeks truth he will find it."

Cadel was trying to offer an olive branch. But Deyva had a different experience with the humans of New Atlanta. She had been exiled by the Order many years ago.

She shot back, "What's the Order say about sea folk and truth?"

Demetris ever the diplomat, "I think what she means to say is, what are you doing here?"

Denton this time answered, "We have many wrongs to make up for. Right now we are trying to find a way to help."

Cadel stood next to his wife, "Come be our guests."

Cadel and Janice motioned toward the center of

the deck which had a three-hundred and sixty degree view of the area. There was a table with some refreshments and snacks.

Deyva again, "Why would we, answer the question?"

Denton turned to her and leaned closer, "I think we can help you find Hanno."

It was a full moon off the southern coast of Sao Miguel near Vila Franca do Campo. Just west of the main port the clear blue water started to move. Then slowly two heads surfaced. It was Demetris and Deyva. They came up out of the water like two navy seals. Their tentacles busy working under the water while they looked around above. East of them and east of the port was a beach front. The main battle cruiser of Blav was parked on the beach.

Demetris into a PDA, "Are sure the fleet cannot detect us?"

Denton from within the Cheonia, "Yes the same primary signal they used to attack us, is still up and running."

Denton had a devise that was obviously New Atlanta tech. It looked like a laptop with multiple projected virtual screens. But then was wired into the computer of the Cheonia. Denton was looking at the Cheonia screens. The controls of the primary signal was up. Showing all vessels. Many of the Malrac fleet was still on patrols along the US coast of the Atlantic. But most were moving toward the other floating cities in Europe and Asia. Closer to Sao Miguel was only Blav's command ship. Denton had a live feed from their transport ship. The Malrac transport ship was parked hovering about twenty feet off the ground at Ermida de Nossa Senhora da Paz or Chapel of our lady of Peace. The chapel was built in 1764 and was up on the hills overlooking the entire island. There was a unique stair case that led up to the chapel adding to the beauty of the place. Legend had it an image of Mother Mary was found in the caves by shepherds and thus it was quickly identified as a sacred space. Hanno was being led out of the transport ship. He was bound with his arms behind him and guarded on both sides. Blav was leading the group into the chapel. Through a series of doors and then down into the caves beneath the chapel deep into the hills.

Denton then added, "We've got Hanno. He is being led into the Chapel just above the city."

Demetris acknowledged, "Copy that."
Demetris and Deyva moved toward a sea wall. As they slowly stepped out of the sea their tentacles turned to legs and their skin turned from blue to a dark pink matching the residents of the island. Not much had changed in Vila Franca do Campo in the last several thousands of years. The narrow streets were still lined with two story all white stone buildings. Both Demetris and Deyva skin changed further camouflaging their bodies with cloth looking material. Although they still had their weapons and tactical armor from a distance

they appeared as a local couple taking a midnight stroll. They made it two blocks up Rua dos Oleiros until they made it to Bento de gois square. The square had the most unique trees in the opening of several buildings. The buildings at the square looked like buildings in Switzerland. Here they commandeered several scooters. But they were electric and floated on a dark red energy source called diwycin, developed by the Malracs. A sign the Malracs had traded with the island for some time. They were quiet but a little too bright for a stealth operation. But they were running out of time.

Down in the caves Blav, the guards, and Hanno came out of a narrow corridor. The small cave opened up into a vault. It was large and circular in shape. Here were many more Malracs making preparations. There was a large hole in the center of the vault that went straight down into the earth. The whole vault was lit up with Malrac spotlights. On the vault walls were writings similar to Hanno's chest designs. There were pictures and writings carved into the stone. But what caught Hanno's eyes was on the far wall. Hanging over the hole was a large section of wall that showed a carving of him. It was him in full Lua expression with all of his tentacles out and his whole body surrounded by the Boya.

The smaller Malrac scientist that had been studying Hanno was at a stone platform near the carved wall and also near the great hole. Blav moved several researchers out of the way.

"Dr. Kronos have you figured out how to work the device?"

He had an assortment of tech both Lua and Malrac that surrounded the stone tablet.

"Well clearly he is the key to opening the gate. But how to insert that key is the question?"

Hanno was close enough to listen in.

"How about if we just chop him up and insert his material into the device?" Blav said coldly.

Hanno eyes opened wide and looked to the guards hoping for some sort of compassion but he found none.

"No no that won't work. It would appears that he has to willingly use his own energy to power it."

Blav turned to the guards, "Untie him."

They looked at him question the order, "Now!"

Demetris and Deyva made it to the top of the hill. They dismounted and uncloaked from their human appearances. They were on the west side of the chapel on the opposite side of the transport ship. There were a number of very large Dacacian guards patrolling the grounds and near the opening of the ship. One was up on the upper back walkway overlooking the staircase. He held a large rifle made from Malrac tech but also had a spear attached to his back. Demetris moved so fast and smooth. His legs appeared to be somewhere between tentacles and human legs with a metamorphous that combined the two into one. He glided silently without making a sound. The guard heard nothing as Demetris pulled his double Trachanjan short swords from his back scabbard. He made quick work first cutting the beast's hamstrings crippling him and then precise stabs to his back that killed him. He moved the guard silently into the tall grass. When Demetris stood on the balcony another guard rounded the corner. He raised his rifle and the energy could be seen to be building in the weapon before a sleek silver arrow pierced his head dropping him. Deyva was on the other side of the courtyard holding a sleek blue green Lua bow. They moved together into the chapel.

"I hope we are not too late." Deyva whispered.

Demetris lightly grabbed her hand, "Have faith my love."

They made their way into the caves and eventually found themselves at the opening to the great vault. There was a Malrac scientist standing over the stairs at the opening taking measurements of the vaulted cave. Blue tentacles surrounded him from behind. One cupping his face and mouth. And several more grabbing his arms and body lifting and silently pulling him back into the darkness. Demetris and Deyva finished him and move to the opening. Down at the center of the cave, Dr. Kronos had Hanno up on the edge of the opening.

They can hear him badgering him.

"Turn on your life source."

Hanno with confidence turned to Blav, "You will have to kill me. I am not helping you in any way."

Blav glided toward him. Even though Hanno was on a ledge that was several feet above the ground Blav changed from his human like appearance to his dark sinister one. He grew right in front of Hanno's eyes from six foot tall to eight feet tall. His legs transformed into six long menacing tentacles. Malracs were very different than Luas. If Luas were humanoid octopuses, Malracs were the giant vampire squids. Blav according to custom was the largest and strongest among their tribe. His dark hood opened up and several other smaller slimy tentacles fished around his bright red eye. Now Hanno saw his face in fullness for the first time. Blav did not have a human like face. Below his one red eye and in place of a nose two vertical slots. In place of a mouth was a sharp squid like beak surrounded by razor sharp serrated teeth. In the center of the beak were two radulas that moved within as he spoke.

"You might think differently if I had your little Moon here."

At that he struck a chord. Hanno jumped of the ledge and stood right up to Blav. He changed into his tentacles and stood on them making him almost at tall as Blav allowing him to look into his eye. His body was flexed and no longer camouflaging as a human. He looked powerful. Blav noticed it too. Blav lowered slightly and turned to the doc but still speaking to Hanno.

"Well I heard she was buried under a million piles of concrete and metal when we destroyed New Atlanta."
He then laughed a dark evil laugh. Hanno changed back and lowered his head. He had not heard. Blav turned back to him.

"Maybe she survived. But you could live up to your destiny and honor her death by helping us all get back to Syrena. Isn't that what you want?"
At that moment Hanno remembered how Blav had killed his parents. This combined with the thought of losing Moon he felt his vengeance rise up in him. In an instant Blav moved so fast. He stood on his back two tentacles and grabbed and threw Hanno with his front two.

Dr. Kronos just murmured, "Um that's a little drastic. Not sure that will work."
As Hanno fell into the abys.

Deyva saw it and almost couldn't hold back, "NOooo!"
Hanno unfurled his tentacles and was trying to grab at the walls on all sides. The diameter of the hole was ten feet wide and just out of his reach. He was hundreds of feet into the darkness. Suddenly he was able to grab hold of a notch in the stone. Deyva's and Demetris burst toward him. They went into a full on attack. Both of them moved like Demetris had moved earlier. There was twenty

guards and scientists in the vault. They moved and attacked them with fluidity and were so coordinated they almost looked like one large beast. Demetris stabbed one guard, while Deyva shot two back to back with her bow. Then they without looking, grabbed tentacles and pulled and switched and resumed the attack on opposite sides. They moved down the stairs and around the lower cave with violence. Several Dacacians got off shots but not one landed. Demetris pulled his large laser flintlock from his lower back and blue energy blasts filled the cave. Hanno had one tentacle wrapped around the notch in the stone. Two tentacles pushing on the other side but the stone was slick. He was using his arms and other tentacles trying to position himself. He was getting frustrated. One part of him would slip after each and he didn't have long. Demetris and Deyva had worked their way through all of the enemies and were now at Blav. Demetris had his gun pointed right at Blav's head holding him in place as Deyva looked over the edge. Her Lua eyes could see deep down into the darkness and she could just barely see Hanno. From the darkness she first saw a small blue then orange glow. The light energy rose brighter and brighter. The glow became so powerful that even Demetris and Blav paused their square off and moved to the edge to see. Hanno's Plava Boya arced from his chest markings causing all of the signs to glow throughout his body. He turned the most beautiful blue, red, then bright hot orangish yellow like a solar burst of the sun. He was no longer holding onto the sides. The energy lined the walls and filled the cracks between the stones. It moved and wound through the rocks and stones and filled the hole with light and energy. Then it was as if the chasm was designed for his energy and it started feeding off of it. The bursts were rhythmically exploding in cycles. So much so that the three observers above had to shield their eyes and step back from the hole. Blav stepped back and fell behind the other two's notice. He noticed the energy had also risen up to the stone tablet and the controls had come alive. He saw something the others didn't. He moved quickly and hid behind a large stone up against the back wall. Then there was a surge like no other and the whole vault was filled with light. Then one last burst and an explosion of light knocked Demetris and Deyva off their feet. They were completely knocked out. From behind the stone Blav saw the cave was illuminated in orange and yellow light but the bursts had stopped. He moved into the opening and all of the carvings and signs on the cave walls were lit up. There at his feet was Hanno also unconscious. He snatched him up and threw him over his shoulder. Blav then moved to the panel, touched and moved several pieces in the controls. And the image of the gate on the wall appeared to come to life and started to open. But it wasn't the gate itself but an ancient visual of the large gate out at sea.

Blav was on the move. Up the cave vault and into the smaller cave making his way up to the chapel. Out of the chapel and to the transport ship. He passed several of his guards and kept moving. Into the ship he flopped Hanno. Demetris and Deyva came out the chapel right as Blav's ship was flying down the mounting toward the command cruiser.

Demetris into his PDA, "Denton we think Blav turned on our gate but he has Hanno."

Denton also saw it on his screen, "Let me see what I can do."

Denton to Nerwin, "Head toward the ship."

"Yes sir."

The Cheonia came to life and started racing toward the ship on the other side of the port. Blav's transport landed near the command ship. Demetris and Deyva were on the scooters and not far behind. Several Dacacians guards came out the back ramp of the Command ship. The Command ship was parked parallel to the ocean and thus the ramp was on the beach facing the port. Right as Blav exited, Hanno had come to. He was weak but aware as Blav had him wrapped in one of his tentacles dragging him in the sand. Guards arrived setting up a perimeter around Blav. Out of nowhere Balene exploded up out of the ocean with so much force that she flew and landed forcefully right on top of several guards. In the same movement she spit out a huge pile of fish, krill, and sea trash. Out of the pile Moon stood up full of whale saliva and fish goo. She held up her small laser side arm. Karkalec was at her side with claws out.

"Let go of my Boyfriend you dirty scoundrel!"

Hanno smiled the biggest smile and laughed and cried simultaneously.

All he could say was, "That's my girl."

She met him with a smile too. They jumped into each other's arms. And Blav made a move and Moon quickly raised the gun, "Oh no you don't."

A large contingent of Luas and Humans arrived on numerous ships at the same time Demetris and Deyva arrived. Blav's men were over whelmed. Then behind them a great burst of air exploded out of the volcanic cone at the center of the Vila Franca Islet. The air was mixed with sea water and water vapors. It exploded high up into the air past the clouds. There was a deep rumbling that shook the ground. Then out of the volcanic cone a vortex of water formed. As soon as it formed, it was like someone turned on a firehose full force. A cyclone of water burst upward to the sky. And kept going until it reached far into space. The water wormhole was now stable. The circumference of the water lined up to the walls of the cone. Demetris and Deyva's eyes were full of tears.

"It's our way home."

They shared a hug. Moon smiled and held Hanno's hand with joy. But then she saw her family as their ship landed on the sand. She ran to her family and greeted them warmly with a hug.

"Daddy, momma!"

Then she punched Brody with a playful punch in the shoulder, "Loser, good to see you."

They all smiled. All of the Luas with hast moved to their ships. And all around the island ships and sea creatures could be seen to enter the cyclone. As the first ship entered it instantly was taken into the cyclone and energized and then disappeared as fast as light as the wormhole sucked it in. Demetris and Deyva headed toward the Cheonia and Nerwin could be seen on its ramp waiting.

Demetris called out, "Hanno come on."

Hanno was locked on the beach looking at Moon. His eyes unmoving. Moon looked at him and then back to her father. The Commander of the city security. The leader of the Bliss Security Council. A third degree Officer in the Order's upper circle. And the controlling domineering father that watched and controlled her every move as a child.

All she could say was, "Daddy please" so softly and so deeply.

Cadel was not the same man. He had changed. He just hugged her and kissed her.

"Go."

She smiled the biggest smile and ran to Hanno. He was still a little weak. And she was still a little slimy.

"I thought I was the one that smelled like fish geesh stinky."

Hanno blushed, "Shut up you. Here now you can smell like me."
She grabbed him in a huge hug but then almost hurt him as she lay a slimy kiss on him. The sun was just starting to come up over the horizon. They boarded the Cheonia. More and more troops from New Atlanta and other allied cities arrived. Blav and his men were disarmed and taken into custody. The Cadel watched from the beach as the Cheonia entered into the Cyclone and then disappeared up into the wormhole. As it did the gate closed and the cyclone fell from the sky splashing down. All that was left was the sun over the sea.

ABOUT THE AUTHOR

Daniel J. Nesher

Daniel has been writing since he was thirteen years old. He has spent his life in service to the public and now has turned to his creative side. Professionally he has been a Sunday School Teacher, Mental health Counselor, Intelligence Officer, Threat Assessor, and Detective. And now he creates worlds :)

BOOKS BY THIS AUTHOR

The Orb Pulpit: Part One Polar Ice

The Orb Pulpit is a three part story of JD Sterling and his path from paranoia to prophet.

The Orb Pulpit: Part Two Tendrils Of The Fiends

The Orb Pulpit: Part Three Full Of Faith And Power